C Holland

**Aspasia**

C Holland

**Aspasia**

ISBN/EAN: 9783744649414

Printed in Europe, USA, Canada, Australia, Japan

Cover: Foto ©Andreas Hilbeck / pixelio.de

More available books at **www.hansebooks.com**

# ASPASIA.

BY

## C. HOLLAND.

PHILADELPHIA:

J. B. LIPPINCOTT & CO.

1869.

# INTRODUCTION.

A PREFACE to my autobiography seems superfluous. It is not for glory that I give my readers a history of my life's experiences, and not that I am to be held up as an ensample in all that is good; but it is that I may, if possible, be instrumental in arousing the latent energies in the minds of some of my readers, that they may gain courage to meet and successfully overcome the trials that shall come upon them, and learn to count them as blessings in disguise, and thus be strengthened in daily duties, be prepared to cope with grim adversity, when it comes, for come it may. To obtain the sweets of real happiness from prosperity, learn to appreciate the society of the virtuous and refined; to discriminate between truth and error; to judge correctly of character, and thus be better fitted to mingle in society, and also understand the true philosophy of living, that will bring the highest degree of permanent happiness. If I shall be instrumental in thus leading even one into paths of virtue and happiness, then am I amply rewarded for my work.

THE AUTHOR.

CHICAGO, May, 1869.

( iii )

# ASPASIA.

## CHAPTER I.

IT was on a beautiful afternoon in June, toward the close of the day, as I was sauntering home from school. The golden rays of a summer's sun were glancing through the forests, and the luxuriant foliage by the wayside was ever and anon casting its heavy shades across my path. The thrush, hidden in the thick underbrush, was warbling its notes of praise; the beautiful red-crested robins, perched upon the high branches of the stately maples and elms that overhung the road, were exultingly singing their evening songs. The sprightly little red squirrel, as innocent, apparently, as though the whole earth were an Eden, would occasionally jump across my path, the lowing of the herd or the soft bleating of the flock could be heard across the meadows, and all nature around me seemed to be full of life, beauty, and love.

Who has not been a child?—although it is said there are no children nowadays, there were children when I was young;—and who has not, in the tender years of childhood, when the emotions of the soul were readily awakened, when love was ardent, when everything beautiful and lovely from without was readily photographed

1*                    (5)

upon the soul, and shown forth with peculiar brilliancy in the animated life,—who, of all such, has not experienced the holy and heavenly influences coming through nature from nature's God? And who does not love to be carried back in their recollections to the scenes of their childhood, when, in the early morning, while the dew was yet heavy on the grass about the door, a happy family were called to the breakfast-table, and, after having partaken of the plain·but substantial fare, the honored head of the household would read a chapter from the old family Bible, and, all reverently bowing around the family altar, he would render devout thanksgiving for the tender watch-care of a kind, heavenly Father "during the dark and defenseless hours of the past night," and supplicate God's favors to rest upon them during the day, —"Give us this day our daily bread." Worship being ended, each would fly to the duties of the day; and, at the time at which I commence my history, mine was to school. Yes, away to school; across the meadow, by the small, beaten path, through the tall herds'-grass and beautiful waving red clover, across the rippling brook, "going on forever," in which the shy, spotted trout were now and then darting out from the deep-shaded water under a log, which lay close under the bank, overgrown with moss, over the hill and across the pasture, where the sprightly little lambs were taking their morning gambols, thus emerging into the road just this side of the "Big Bridge," and so on to the old red school-house which stood under the hill.

My father was a farmer. I have heard him say he had nothing to commence life with but a good common-school education, a well-trained mind, and an abiding faith in God; firmly believing that "the hand of the diligent maketh rich." This was the legacy bequeathed to him by his parents, to which he had a perfect title, the same having been inherited by them; and who would wish for a better?

I have heard my mother say she was also trained in the school of adversity; and, thus united, both my parents felt themselves continually overshadowed by the presence of God, and their everyday acts were squared by the rule of love. Their children were early dedicated to God, and, as they grew up to manhood and womanhood, they were continually, by example and precept, enjoined to "walk in wisdom's ways." My father was known among the neighbors as an upright, honest man; and how many times I have heard him say to "the boys," "In all your dealings be strictly honest."

I was the youngest of my father's family; there were three boys and two girls older than myself, and it was the very month and the very day that I was twelve years old, that I was returning from school, as before mentioned; and being only disturbed in my reflections by the beauty and loveliness of nature around me (and not greatly disturbed, either, for I was every day made familiar with these lovely scenes), I said to myself, "What am I, and what am I to be?"

The first I could easily answer:—I am a girl. Yes, a wild, rollicking girl. The second depended upon my resolve, and the strength of such resolutions; and I then and there resolved that I would be a woman in the broadest sense of the term.

I was conscious of possessing natural endowments which, if cultivated and fully developed, would fit me for usefulness and enable me to fulfill a mission of good.

My brothers and sisters had all enjoyed the advantages of the district school, and John and James, the two eldest, were already grown to manhood, and engaged in business,

John on a farm, and James as clerk in a store in a neighboring village. William, my youngest brother, was in his last term at the academy, and, upon graduating, he came home to remain on the farm with my father. Catherine (or Kate, good soul, as we familiarly called her), my eldest sister, was about to be married to the Rev. Mr. Shaw, a young minister, just licensed to preach, and installed over the church in our town. Elizabeth, my second sister, was in her second year at the Young Ladies' Seminary, in a town about twenty miles distant.

Thus I was the only girl—yes, the only child—then at home.

There was but one house within a half-mile of my father's: that was Deacon Jones's.

Just over the hill, and about half-way to Deacon Jones's, there was a strip of pine woods, and a beautiful brook ran through it and across the road, covered by a rickety old bridge. Here Isabella Jones (Bell, we called her) and myself often met, and, wading into the soft, rippling water, among the smooth stones of the brook, amused ourselves for hours catching the sprightly little minnows, which we accomplished by first scraping out a basin in the sand at the edge of the water, then walling it around with stones from the brook, and " chinking it in with sods," leaving a sort of gate-way or passage on the water-side, then each, with an alder bush in hand, would wade in and drive the little fish into the basin thus prepared, and, stopping the aperture, we would play with them awhile, then let them out, a few at a time, and watch them swiftly gliding down stream, as much as to say, Catch me again if you can.

Bell Jones was about my age, and she had a brother George, a little older than herself. George and my brother William frequently went fishing of a rainy day (when it was so wet they could not work on the farm), and Bell and I used to keep a supply of minnows in our basin for the boys to use as bait for fishing.

During the summer vacation we used often, of a warm afternoon, to meet in the "pine woods" by the brook, and enjoy ourselves either in fishing, or hunting rabbits, for the boys had taught us to hunt and fish; of course we used no fowling-pieces. There were many rabbits in the woods, and Rover, our faithful house-dog, who always attended us in our ramblings about the farm, was an expert in finding and catching them.

The boys also used to set their snares across the rabbit-paths, and thus catch many; and occasionally a partridge, which had foolishly strayed from the covey, would unconsciously "stick her head" in the snare, and away she would go dangling in the air, out of reach of any sly old fox that might be out in search of family supplies to feed her cunning baby foxes in the den.

One very warm day we were playing in the cool brook under the shade of the dense old pines, and suddenly we were startled at the cry of some one; we ran hastily to the road, whence the sound came, and who should we find but Laura Greenwood, a girl about my age, but one we did not meet very often, for the reason that Mr. Greenwood lived nearly a mile east of our house, across the fields, and he was an irreligious man, and neither himself nor his family attended church. Laura had been berrying, and, upon the principle that "the longest way round is the nearest way home," she had come around the road, and as she was passing along leisurely in the shade of the heavy branches of the stately old pines which overhung the road, all at once a huge black snake slid out into the path, directly in front of her, and, raising his ugly head about a foot from the ground, disputed her passage. The poor girl was almost frightened out of her senses. Bell caught a stick and I a stone, and we were just about to move upon the enemy, when Farmer Osgood came suddenly around the turn of the road, driving a yoke of oxen. I beckoned him to stop his team, which he did, then pointed to the snake, and, with one stroke of his heavy ox-whip, he cut it completely in twain. We thanked him for the deliverance, and all three of us went down to the brook.

Of course the subject of conversation was snakes, and each vied with the others in telling snake stories.

At last said I, "Girls, I can beat you both in a snake story,—and it's a true one, too."

"Let's have it, then," said they.

"Well," said I, "we will go out on the grass yonder, under the shade of those sweet-scented locust-trees, and I'll tell the story," which was agreed to; and, after having each picked our aprons full of honeysuckles, and a handful of wintergreens (or, as we called the young plants, "young comeups"), we seated ourselves for the story.

"Now," said Laura, "tell us a true one."

"Yes, I will," said I; "and this is it.

"A great while ago there was a man and his wife lived in a beautiful garden, a perfect paradise of a place, and, according to what I have heard about it, it was something like the place where we are, only it was a thousand times more beautiful; but there were three little rivers running through it, just like Jones's Brook through this hollow; and we have plenty of honeysuckles here, but in the garden in which this man and woman lived there were all sorts of beautiful flowers, the perfumes of which made it perfectly delightful living there, and everything was just as lovely as it could be. The owner of the garden gave it to this man, and told him that he need not work at all, but only be happy——"

"And his wife, too?" inquired Laura.

" Yes, and his wife also ; she need not work at all, but only be happy; and he would give them all there was there, and furnish them with all the food they wanted, if they would obey him.

" Now surely that was very reasonable, was it not?

" Well, there were a great many fruit trees in the garden (for it was a large place, I suppose; bigger than my father's farm), and the owner of the place told the man and woman that they might pick and eat just as much fruit as they wished, and welcome. But right in the middle of the garden there stood a tree that hung full of splendid-looking fruit, large and fair, the sides of which were red and tempting, but deadly poison ; and the owner of the place told the man and his wife that they must not touch the fruit of that tree, and I presume it was because it was poisonous; for you know that some of the prettiest wild flowers and berries we find are poison to touch or eat. Well, the man and his wife, in walking around, had to go right past this tree very often; and every time they saw it they wanted some of the fruit.

" There were a great many animals, of every sort, that the owner of the place had kept tame ; and they walked about the garden as much as they pleased, and without hurting each other, or the man and woman, of whom they were very fond.

" There were lions, tigers, bears, cattle, horses, sheep, dogs, and every other animal that can be thought of. And there was a very beautiful serpent——"

" Oh," said Laura, " beautiful serpent! how can you say so?"

" Well," said I, "it was beautiful then ; it didn't crawl

along on the ground, as it does now, but stood up, I suppose; perhaps it had feet, so that it could walk and hold its head high in the air; and you know very well that if we didn't dislike snakes as we do, we should have called that big black snake, that frightened you so to-day, handsome.

"Well, this old serpent was one day at the tree that bore such beautiful fruit, when the man and his wife passed along, and said the serpent, 'Why don't you eat some of the delicious fruit on this tree?'"

Then the girls both burst out laughing. "Why," said Bell, "we thought you were going to tell us a true story."

"So I am," said I.

"Then why say the serpent talked?"

"Because he did," said I; "and it is supposed by many people that nearly all, if not all, the animals could once speak, and not only converse with each other, but with man; and we know that they have a sort of language by which they talk with each other now. Dr. Woodman and Parson Shaw were at our house last week, and I heard them talking with my father about this very thing. And Dr. Woodman said that several of the animals have the organs of speech fully developed now, showing that they did once speak. 'Yes,' said Parson Shaw, 'and I believe that when sin is all gone out of the world, the animals will talk again.'"

"Sin!" said Laura; "what does he mean by that?"

"He means," said I, "when all wicked people die, or else become good, so that nobody lies, or cheats, or swears, or steals, or does anything wrong.

"But to my story. The man and woman told the serpent that the owner of the garden charged them not to eat of that fruit, and that if they did they should surely die.

"The serpent then asked them what they supposed such beautiful fruit was made to grow for, if not to be eaten, and right in the midst of the garden, too, where they passed every day; 'and besides,' said he, 'I know you will not surely die if you eat of the fruit of this tree.' But the man went on, and wouldn't stop to talk with the serpent; and it had been better if the woman had gone also; but she did not; she liked to hear the serpent talk; he had sparkling eyes, was smooth-tongued, and flattered her; told her she would be like a god, know everything, if she would listen to him and eat the fruit. And she finally yielded to the temptation, and picked some splendid specimens of the fruit from the tree, and ate them, and she was filled with ecstasies of delight, and ran after her husband, and gave him some, and he ate it, and they both went to dancing and acting shamefully.

"The serpent stood looking on to see the effect, for he knew he had lied to them, and that it would prove the ruin of both of them. Well, it was toward evening, and they were acting in this manner, but were beginning to feel anxious lest the owner of the garden would find it out; and all at once they heard the man's name called, and they ran and hid themselves in the bushes; but the owner of the garden called loudly to them, to know why they had hidden from him; then the man confessed that he had eaten of that forbidden fruit, but said he should not have done so if his wife had not eaten and given him some, and then his wife said she would not have done so had it not been for the serpent.

"Then the owner of the garden cursed the serpent, and said he should crawl on the ground, and eat dust always, and that everybody should hate it, and should bruise its head, and kill it. And that's what makes us hate snakes so.

"And the owner drove the man and his wife right out of the garden, and put one of his servants, with a sword in his hand, at the gate to keep them out, poor, forlorn, despised creatures; and the animals ran after them, and scared them; before this, all the animals loved them, and would eat grass out of their hands; but now the cattle stuck forward their ears, and ran bellowing after them. The asses brayed after them, and scared them nearly to death. The dogs barked after them, and would have bitten them, had they not lain down just under the gate, where the servant with the sword in his hand stood. But they were kept awake all night by the howling of wolves and roaring of lions, and thus the poor wretches very soon came to realize the terrible consequences of doing wrong."

"Well," said the girls, "this is a pretty big story."

Bell said she thought she had heard something like it, but could not say certain. Laura said she had never heard anything at all like it, and she was a little inclined to disbelieve it.

"Now," said they, "tell us the name of the owner of the garden, and the name of the man and his wife, and where it was, and we will believe it."

Said I, "It is almost night now, and we will meet here next Saturday afternoon, and then I'll tell you; but, in the mean time, you ask your parents if they ever heard the story."

Said Laura, "Mr. Osgood, who lives near our house, has a beautiful daughter, Mary, about as old as we are; and, if you girls do not object, I would like to bring her with me on Saturday."

I replied that we should be delighted to see her.

So, bidding each other good-by, we ran to our homes.

# CHAPTER II.

THE day was clear and pleasant; the new-mown hay in the meadows filled the air with its fragrance.

My mother, who had been busying herself about the household duties, with what little assistance I was able to render, had finished up her work and sat down to her mending, and I was sitting by the window, reading, when who should come in but Jane Fisher (or Aunt Jane, as she was familiarly called)?

Miss Jane was a maiden lady who lived in the village, and she thought a great deal of my mother, and frequently visited at our house. She was one of those precise women, naturally very jealous and suspecting, very fond of hearing and telling some new thing; she was, however, a good woman, and my mother said she thought she tried to overcome those defects in her nature, and, by the grace of God, she succeeded to a great extent; but she possessed the happy faculty of obtaining a full store of news each time before visiting us.

I heard my mother say to father once, after Miss Jane had left, "that if she could visit us every evening we should be quite as well off for news, living on the farm, as if we were residing in the village, and possibly better, for Jane told her many things she was sure she could not have learned from any other source."

To which my father replied, " Well, I think Jane is a good woman, and means well, and her case only proves to me that we are all designed by Providence to fill a par-

ticular niche in life; in other words, it requires all sorts
of people to make a world.

"And although some may be afraid of Jane, because of
her everlasting gabbling, yet, after all, I think she is a
very valuable member of society; for if she sees or hears
of the slightest departure from duty of one of the members of the church, whether male or female, young or old,
she runs right to the minister with it; and if there is a
young gentleman or lady about to be married, and Jane
hears anything serious against the character of either, she
runs right straight to the other and reports it, and it is
getting so that people in town dare not do wrong, lest
Jane will know it; and, although it is in many in-
stances very annoying to have such a person about, yet
I think, on the whole, society is the better for their presence."

"Well," said my mother, "good-afternoon, Jane. How
do you get along this warm day?"

"Oh, dear," said she, "I am about melted; give me a
fan. I have come afoot all the way from town, and there's
Alex. Fish and Mary Bacon came whirring by me in a top
buggy; plenty of room for me to ride, but they didn't
ask me; and I have heard something about that young
Fish that I don't think is exactly right, and they say
Mary Bacon is trying—oh, how hot 'tis!—they say Mary
is trying with all her might to catch him, and I intend to
see her, and tell her what I have heard, and put her on
her guard; it's really none of my business, but then
Mary is a good girl, and I feel as though it was my
duty."

My mother replied, "Jane, you had better be careful,
or you will get Mrs. Bacon offended with you; for my
opinion is she thinks very well of young Fish."

"Well," said Jane, "I can't help it if she does; I must

do my duty. By the way, what do you think of Parson Shaw's sermon last Sabbath?"

"In what respect?" inquired my mother.

"Why, the doctrine of salvation by grace."

My mother replied, "I like it; and it is, indeed, a precious doctrine to me to feel that, with all my sins resting upon me, I can cast the burden all upon Jesus, who has said, 'My grace shall be sufficient for you.'"

"Oh, yes," replied Jane; "but then it strikes me we have got something to do. I believe in works some. There are lots of Christians who are delighted to hear the minister preach against works, and of a salvation purely by grace, for no other reason in the world but that they are too lazy to work, and haven't enough religion to make them."

"No doubt," replied my mother, "there are too many such church-members as you describe; but, Jane, you must bear this in mind, those who are truly Christians, have the love of Christ in their hearts, have been born again by the Spirit of God, and renewed in the spirit of their mind by grace divine,—all such will work; no power on earth can keep them from working. The Bible says our faith is only manifested by our works, and if we have no works it is a sure evidence that we have no faith, for 'faith without works is dead.'"

"Well," said Jane, "I think you are about right, after all; I never looked at it in just that light before."

During all this conversation I had been as mute as a statue; but the principles of theology which had been under discussion were of great importance to me, and finding that a sermon, which I heard, but did not remember a single sentence of, was of so much interest to ladies of mature years, I resolved that henceforth I would pay particular attention to all the preacher should say, and try to remember it, which I have ever since done, and greatly to my benefit, and by the time I was sixteen years of age I could remember and repeat one-half of any sermon I heard; and if my young readers would all accustom themselves to this practice, they would find it very interesting and vastly profitable.

After the conversation just mentioned, Jane turned her chair around toward me, and inquired after my health, whether I attended school or not, how far advanced I was in my studies, etc., and, said she, with a deep-drawn sigh, "Oh, dear! when I see a bright little girl like you just emerging out of girlhood, I pity her, for she don't realize the real happiness of youth, nor the troubles of mature life, and I recall the lines of the old poet:

"Seek not the sweets of life, in life's first bloom;
They ill prepare us for the pain to come."

To which beautiful sentiment I replied, I enjoyed the sweets of life every day; that only yesterday "us girls" were down in the pine woods by Jones's Brook, and we had a splendid time, but then I didn't suppose these pleasures could prepare us for the adversities of life, which I felt were sure to come upon all, as I had frequently heard my father say.

Just at this time sister Kate came down-stairs; she and Miss Jane met each other cordially, and about the first question Jane asked was to know of Kate when she was to be married; she said she couldn't help thinking about it in church every Sunday; it was a good match, and she was glad of it; she felt as though it was providential.

Kate replied, she had not certainly fixed upon the day of the wedding, but assured Jane that if any one out of the family was invited she should be.

At this, Jane sprang out of her chair, and, said she,

"Kate, you're the best girl that ever was born in this town," and tears of gratitude filled her eyes.

"Well," said Kate, "you ought not to think of our being married, during the services on the Sabbath."

"I suppose I ought not," said Jane, "but I can't help it; for your mother knows I always thought everything of you, ever since you were a little girl; and as for Parson Shaw, I do think if ever there was a saint on earth he is one. I was over to Mr. Brown's the other night when his little boy died, and it seemed as though it would kill Mr. and Mrs. Brown; they fairly worshiped that little boy. Parson Shaw was there, and it certainly seemed as though I never heard such a prayer as he made, and such consolation as he poured into those wounded hearts I never heard before. I just ran over to Mr. Brown's this morning to see if they had anything to say about it, for I knew you would like to hear it, and I knew they would say something about it; and I hadn't more than entered the house when Mrs. Brown burst out crying, and, said she, 'Jane, did you ever hear a minister talk and pray as Mr. Shaw did when Johnny died? husband and I both said it seemed as though he was an angel.'"

Just at this time Peggy, the kitchen girl, announced tea; my father coming in from the field, we all gathered around the tea-table, and Jane kept father so busy talking that we did not finish tea till dark; then father called one of the hired men, and he hitched up one of the horses, and took Jane home. And, as she was getting in the wagon, said mother, "Come again, Jane; we love to have you come and see us."

"Yes," said I, "because you have so much news to tell."

"Hush!" said my mother. "You should not tell the

truth at all times, though you should always speak the truth."

The morrow was the Sabbath; we all sat about the table, and read from our Bibles the chapter containing the Sabbath-school lesson, and, having read the same, my father expounded it to us all, verse by verse, after which worship was held, and we all retired to rest.

Sabbath dawned upon us a lovely day, and in due time we all rode to church. The house was full, and the congregation was deeply affected. Father said he did not remember of having heard a more impressive discourse than Mr. Shaw preached that day. His text was, "Except ye repent, ye shall all likewise perish;" and it is said that Farmer Osgood, Mrs. Greenwood, and several others, who had never been to church in this town, were there, and they were all deeply affected, and some even shed tears. The pastor referred to Johnny Brown's sudden death, and warned all the children to repent of their sins, and love Jesus, so that if any of them were called to die suddenly, as Johnny Brown had, they might not perish, but have everlasting life. He then appealed to parents to attend more earnestly to the interests of the souls of their children. I remember with what pathos he urged upon parents their duties in this respect, and how he wept when he said, with his eyes turned toward heaven, "My dear friends, one and all, I expect, sooner or later, to stand before yonder white throne, and render an account of my stewardship here; and, oh, how blessed it will be, and how my Saviour will rejoice, and how angels will sing, if I can be permitted to hand in every name of those who now listen to my voice as among those who 'have washed their robes white in the blood of the Lamb'!"

I shall never lose the impressions received that day; and, although I had previously resolved to lead a Christian's life, my resolutions were greatly strengthened that day.

My father was superintendent of the Sabbath-school, and, after the lesson was over, he called the school to order, and spoke of little Johnny Brown's death (for he was a member of the Sabbath-school, and greatly beloved by all). My father said that when Johnny was dying he sent word to all the little boys and girls in the Sunday-school to love their Saviour, and be good, and meet him in heaven.

He said Johnny was so happy that he was going home to his Saviour that he sang the following, and begged of those who stood about his bed to continue to sing to him as long as he lived :

"And may I still get there,
   Still reach the heavenly shore ;
The land forever bright and fair,
   Where sorrow reigns no more.

"I part with earth and sin,
   And shout, The danger's past,
My Saviour takes me fully in,
   And I am his at last."

There was scarcely a dry eye when father finished reading the hymn, and some of the children sobbed aloud ; it was deeply solemn, and many resolved from that time to lead better lives.

As usual, dinner was ready for us at home when we returned from church, and we had but just been seated at the table when Laura Greenwood came running up the yard, past the window before which the table stood. On seeing her I ran to meet her, and, perceiving by her down-cast look that something sad had happened, inquired hastily what was the matter. She was so out of breath with running that she could hardly speak, but, said she, "When we were returning from church to-day, my father's horse got frightened, and ran away, and threw us all out of the wagon, and somehow I escaped; but I expect it broke both my parents' limbs, for they lie there beside the road, and they cannot get up. And, oh, I am so sorry! because they have not been to church for many years, and had it not been for me they would not have gone to-day."

My father heard Laura's story, and arose quickly from the table, and said he to the hired man, "Jump on to the black horse, and run for Dr. Woodman, and tell him to go to Mr. Greenwood's as quick as possible, and I will be there." Then, catching up his hat, he ran across the fields to Mr. Greenwood's with all possible speed, and mother and Kate followed as fast as they could, taking Laura with them.

My father found Mr. and Mrs. Greenwood lying by the side of the road, near their house, where they had been thrown. They were groaning with pain; on examination, he became satisfied their limbs were fractured, and he could not, without assistance, get them into the house. Soon, however, mother and Kate reached there, and soon after the doctor and hired man, and they took them into the house, and laid them on separate beds, and the doctor, assisted by my father (who, by the way, was more than half a doctor or surgeon himself), soon reduced the fracture and bound up their bruises. Father then went for the horse, caught him, and put him in the field. He then went to work and did the chores about the house and barn, and mother and Kate took care of the invalids that night.

As father had as much as he could possibly do on his farm at home, and consequently could not spend any portion of his time at Mr. Greenwood's, he went in the morning and hired a man and his wife, most excellent people, to go there and take care of them, and do the work about the house.

In the afternoon of that very day Parson Shaw was riding past. Father stopped him, and related the sad occurrence. He said that although Mr. Greenwood had scoffed at religion, still, if my father thought advisable, he would call on them; and father encouraged him by all means to do so.

On the next day Mr. Shaw called on them, and found them suffering great pain; he gave them a few words of cheer and consolation, and was about to leave them, when Mr. Greenwood earnestly requested him to remain, as he had something to say to him. Said he, " I have not been inside of a church before for twenty years, and now, by going last Sunday, this terrible accident has happened to both wife and me. My first thought, when hurt, was to curse the church, minister and all, but something seemed to operate on my mind which prevented it; wife said, 'There! if it hadn't been for your persistency in going to church we should not have been injured;' but, somehow (and it seemed strange), I couldn't answer as she expected I would, and now your coming here to see us to-day is another choker for me."

Mr. Shaw then asked him how he happened to go to church last Sabbath. He replied, " I shouldn't if it had not been for Laura. A few days since she met Aspasia Horton and Bell Jones, and spent an afternoon with them, and the girls were telling stories; Aspasia told them the story of the fall of man in the garden of Eden, and, either because it was told in Aspasia's peculiar style, or something else, it made such an impression upon Laura that she told it all anew to wife and me, and insisted upon knowing who the man and woman were, and where it was, and said we must know all about it, for Aspasia said our parents would know, and we must ask them. Says wife, 'James, go and get the old Bible, and read it all to Laura.' I asked her where it was; I did not know that we had one in the house; she said it was up garret, in an old chest, with some papers of no value. Laura ran at once and brought it, and I read to her the whole history, and somehow a strange sensation came over us all. Laura inquired what effect the curse upon Adam had on us, and I was compelled to say that the ministers said we were all in consequence sinners, and under the curse of the law, and under condemnation of death because of our sins; 'but,' said I, 'I do not believe one word of it,' while I did believe it, and feared in consequence. 'Well,' said Laura, 'the Bible is true, isn't it?' I replied, 'Yes, I suppose so.' 'Well, then, I should think it was high time that we were all doing something to get rid of our sins.' At this remark I had a strange feeling come over me, and I could not resist the conviction that I was a sinner, and the more I thought of it the worse I felt, until I spoke to my wife about it, and she said she had a strange feeling come over her also; 'but, law me!' said she, 'it's all foolishness, and we better banish all such thoughts from our minds at once. Laura has been with Aspasia Horton until she has got her head completely turned, and if we don't look out she will make us just as foolish.' But, somehow (continued Mr. Greenwood), I could not throw off my feelings, and last Saturday night, when we sat down to the supper-table, said Laura, 'Pa, why don't you ask a blessing upon the food, same as Mr. Horton and Deacon Jones do?' This was a stumper; I was feeling bad enough before, and rising from the table suddenly, as though I did not hear her, I said to wife, 'You need not wait for me; I must go before dark and see whether I locked the barn-doors or not.' I went to the barn, and, dropping upon

my knees, cried, 'God be merciful to me a sinner;' this I
repeated several times, and returned to the house, and
somehow I felt better than I ever did before ; this was
(so far as my recollection serves me) the first time I ever
prayed.   On returning to tea, said Laura, ' Pa, are we all
going to Mr. Shaw's church to-morrow ?'   ' Yes,' said I,
' we shall, if we live.'  ' No, we sha'n't do any such thing,'
said my wife.   I made no reply, and Laura burst out
crying; and finally her mother said if she would stop
crying we would all go to church ; and I thank God
that we did, though this terrible accident has happened,
for there I heard those precious truths preached by you,
the declaration of Jesus, ' I am the way, the truth, and
the life,' and that precious truth, ' My grace shall be sufficient for you.'   Oh, I tell you, Parson Shaw, I have been
a great sinner, and while you were preaching that sermon I gave myself to Jesus, and dedicated everything I
have to him, and resolved to live and die a Christian.
But in coming home, I regret to say, my wife was very
petulant, and found a great deal of fault with you, and
with me for going to church, and said she'd never go
again ; and then Laura commenced crying, and finally
wife told her to stop, and she would go again next Sunday.   I felt sure that the Spirit of God was at work on
her mind, and I silently prayed for her conversion. Just
at this time my horse got frightened at a cow that jumped
out of the bushes, and ran, and threw us out; and now
wife says she believes God did it so that we should think
of our sins, and have time, free from the cares of life, to
become Christians."

Mr. Shaw said he never felt more rejoiced in his life,
and he talked with them for two hours, read several chap-
ters in the Bible, and prayed with them.

The next Sabbath Mr. Shaw related the case in church

after sermon, and said that Brother Greenwood (he called him brother, now) had considerable hay that must be cut and gathered in, and he presumed other work that should be done, and asked as many men in his congregation as could possibly leave their business to meet him at Brother Greenwood's house to-morrow (Monday) morning, at eight o'clock, with all the necessary tools for cutting and gathering his hay; and at the appointed time there were about forty men, besides boys, assembled at Mr. Greenwood's, and, under the directions of Parson Shaw, they gathered rapidly in his barn all his hay, and did up all other necessary work.

Mr. and Mrs. Greenwood were confined to the house a long time, and the first place they rode to, after recovering sufficiently to ride, was to church.

And on that very first Sabbath they and Laura all united with the church, and it was an impressive scene; all three were baptized, and besides them there were over forty persons who joined the church that day.

The accident to Mr. and Mrs. Greenwood, and their conversion, was the beginning of a powerful work of grace in our town; almost every family was visited, and some members made the special subjects of grace; and this whole work commenced with the story I told the girls in the pine woods by the brook.

# CHAPTER III.

"Although unconscious of the pleasing charm,
  The mind still bends where friendship points the way;
Let virtue then thy partner's bosom warm,
  Lest vice should lead thy softened soul astray."

SATURDAY came, when Bell, Laura, Mary and I were to meet in the "pine woods by the brook." Owing to her parents' misfortunes, of course Laura could not be there, so Bell and I went to her house; and almost the first words Laura said were, "My father has told me all about the snake story, and says God was the owner of the garden, and the name of it was Eden, and the names of the man and his wife were Adam and Eve; and father and mother both say they are so glad you told us the story."

I asked her why. She said, "because it had been the means of leading them all to the Saviour."

Laura said, also, she didn't feel like playing then, and, besides, she must be with her parents to help nurse them. We both understood her feelings, and our sympathies were drawn out toward her, and we volunteered to assist her in administering comfort to her parents, so far as we were able. Thus we spent the entire day, promising, when we left, to repeat the visit, which we did often during their confinement. Thus an enduring friendship was formed between us, which grew with our growth and increased with our years.

Summer vacation having passed, I again resumed my

( 27 )

studies at the district school, which I continued until spring. Then sister Elizabeth, having completed her studies, returned home, and I afterward entered the same seminary. I should have entered at the fall term, but, as sister Kate was to be married on Thanksgiving, mother said she could not endure to have all her daughters away from home during the winter.

As Thanksgiving drew near, Parson Shaw's visits at our house became more frequent, and about two weeks before Thanksgiving, at a meeting of the sewing-society, at the house of Dr. Goodman, in the village, Jane Fisher took sister Kate aside, and, said she, " We have some private business to talk over, that you had better not hear."

Kate took the hint, and pretended she had an errand at the store, and, as soon as she left, said Jane, " Ladies, I suppose you all know that Parson Shaw and Kate Horton are to be married on Thanksgiving, and in church, too ; the parson has already rented a house, and I think the society ought to furnish it for them, for he is just commencing, and is poor, and his salary of a thousand dollars won't any more than support them, let alone purchase furniture, and certainly there never was a minister who labored more faithfully than he."

This was received with a hearty response by all ; but, said they, " Jane, how do you know they are to be married so soon?"

" How do I know it ?" said she ; " don't I know it, and don't I know all that's going on ?"

" Yes," said Mrs. Bacon, " you do ; if you do not, then you have changed amazingly."

" Well," said Jane, " it is fortunate for you that there is one who keeps posted, and can inform you ladies of what is going on."

"Well," said Mrs. Woodman, "what shall be done?"

Different plans were suggested; and finally a committee of five ladies, with Jane Fisher as chairman, was appointed to call upon the gentlemen of the town the next day and solicit subscriptions, and to meet and report at an adjourned meeting, then to decide upon further action. At that meeting there were twice as many present as there were at the first.

Neither my mother nor Kate knew of the adjourned meeting; the ladies purposely kept it from them; and, had they known it, they would not have been able to be present, as my Uncle and Aunt Horton were visiting us.

The committee, being called on, reported cash subscriptions to the amount of twelve hundred dollars; and, besides this, Mr. Greenwood subscribed ten cords of wood, Farmer Osgood, a new milch cow, and Deacon Jones, two tons of hay.

The ladies were all delighted at their success, as well they might be. A good many things were promised by them besides those donations mentioned.

The questions then arose, what to purchase, and how to get possession of the house without informing the parson, for they intended to take him and Kate by surprise. They finally hit upon the following expedient.

They sent for Mr. Brown, the owner of the house; he came at once, and they stated the case to him. He replied, "I have the keys of the house yet, and I will say to Parson Shaw that he must secure board for himself and wife at Mr. Horton's for a couple of months; and as soon as I get the house fixed for him I will let him know."

"Capital!" they all shouted.

· The committee then proceeded to the business in hand, and before Thanksgiving Day the house was furnished from garret to cellar. Mr. Greenwood had drawn his wood and piled it in the shed; Deacon Jones had put the hay in the barn; and, on Thanksgiving Day, Farmer Osgood drove the cow into the yard.

Our family were all at home that day. There was father, mother, John and his wife and little boy, James, William, Kate, Elizabeth, and myself, also Uncle and Aunt Horton—from New York; and Parson Shaw was also with us at dinner. We all went to church, leaving the girl to roast the turkeys. And, so far as the preaching was concerned, people said it was a great deal better than they supposed it would be under the circumstances.

Directly after the sermon Mr. Shaw came down from the pulpit, and met Kate at the pew-door and escorted her in front of the altar, and they were joined in the holy bands of matrimony by the Rev. Dr. Sprague, from a neighboring town, who had volunteered to perform the ceremony. He was a fast friend of Parson Shaw.

Mother advised Kate to be married in church, and then no one would feel hurt at not being invited to the wedding.

After meeting, Kate asked Jane Fisher to spend the evening at our house; but she declined, saying she was engaged. Soon after arriving at home, dinner was announced, and we all gathered around such a Thanksgiving dinner as none but my mother could prepare. There were fifteen in all, for the Rev. Dr. Sprague and his wife came home from church with us. Many were the innocent jokes at that table, perpetrated at the expense of Kate and Mr. Shaw.

While at the table, Mr. Brown's boy George rode up to the door on horseback, and handed a letter to the kitchen-girl. She brought it to my father, and remarked that the boy would wait for a reply. Father opened the letter, and read it aloud, as follows:

"EDWARD HORTON, ESQ.

"MY DEAR SIR:—For your new son-in-law, my beloved pastor, Rev. Mr. Shaw, I entertain the profoundest regard, and even more, I love him for the brilliancy of his intellect and the depth and ardor of his Christian character; and in this I do but express the sentiments of this entire community. For your daughter Kate, now Mrs. Shaw, I cannot find language to express the admiration and love entertained toward her by all the ladies of the town; and for yourself, and the other members of your family, I need not assure you of my high esteem. Your friends are desirous your entire family should meet us and spend this evening at the house I have rented to Mr. Shaw, and which I intend he shall occupy so soon as it is in fit condition. Quite likely your family and friends will disperse soon after Thanksgiving is over, and it may be interesting to them to know where your daughter is to reside. We will have the house warmed, and try and make it comfortable and pleasant, and shall expect to see you all. ·

"Yours, in behalf of many friends,

"HORATIO BROWN."

While father was reading the letter, I observed side glances being cast, first from mother to Kate, then between Kate and Mr. Shaw, then between Uncle and Aunt Horton, and between the boys and girls.

Finishing the letter, said father, "Mr. Shaw, what do you say?"

He replied, "It is a mystery to me; I do not understand it at all."

But mother winked at Kate, and said she, "I think I do. We will all go."

So father returned a note, saying we should all accept the invitation.

After supper, Kate called mother into "the best room," and said she, "Mother, what do you suppose all this means?"

Said mother, "Kate, don't you remember Jane Fisher wanted to have you leave the sewing-society at Dr. Woodman's? That has something to do with this evening's party; and, if it was not for the very hard times, as I heard your father say, I should expect they were a going to make you and your husband a present; but, the truth is, the people are too poor to expect anything from them, by way of presents, until business revives."

"Oh, yes," replied Kate. "I would not ask one of them for a single penny."

As night came on, the horses were all harnessed and at the door. There were four carriages of us all, so we drove off down the road, through the "pine woods," and as we passed Deacon Jones's, the deacon and his wife and children were just starting out of the yard in their two-horse carriage, and followed us.

Arriving at the house, we found it brilliantly lighted, and it seemed as though the whole town was there. On going in, we were greeted by the church-choir singing a thanksgiving anthem, after which we were shown all over the house, which was furnished thoroughly in every room; crockery and cutlery well stored away upon the pantry shelves; all kitchen arrangements perfect; cellars well stored with potatoes, apples, squashes, etc. We were all led to the wood-shed, where Farmer Greenwood had piled his wood; from here we went to the barn, and saw the sweet herds'-grass, placed in the mow by Deacon

Jones, and the Farmer-Osgood cow was taking her supper from a crib full of the same.

On returning to the house, and being seated in the parlor, Mr. Brown stated "that on behalf of the numerous friends of the Rev. Mr. Shaw and his accomplished and devoted Christian wife, all that they had seen, and one year's lease (free of costs) of the house itself, were here presented to him as a small token of their love."

Mr. Shaw was so completely overwhelmed by this munificence that he sat speechless, and Kate burst into loud sobs, and, indeed, there were but few dry eyes there.

I could not help crying as I saw Kate give way.

After some moments Mr. Shaw rose, and replied, or rather acknowledged the gift, as follows:

" Brother Brown, and each and all of these messengers of love who have contributed either directly or indirectly to this munificent gift, you have taken us so entirely by surprise, and your benefactions are so liberally bestowed, that I feel wholly incompetent to make to you a befitting acknowledgment. Most surely such acts of love can only flow from hearts divested of selfishness, and elevated by affection. I fear we are unworthy of being made the recipients of such distinguished tokens of regard."

"No, you are not," said Jane Fisher, who stood with a tray in her hand, ready to pass round the cake as soon as the parson finished his speech.

He proceeded: " I can only say, further, we thank you, one and all ; and we shall ever labor and pray that the richest of God's blessings may descend and rest upon you, and upon this whole community; and such nobility of soul predominating in society will insure the blessings of Heaven upon you all."

All who could obtain chairs did so ; others stood, and

many were compelled to leave for lack of room in the house.

At about nine o'clock the people all bade Kate and her husband good-night, and left for their homes.

Our family were then left alone, and, after consultation, it was decided that Mr. Shaw and Kate should, from that moment, occupy the house, instead of boarding at our house, as they expected to, and also that Dr. and Mrs. Sprague should spend the night there. This being agreed upon, the rest of us returned home.

So passed that Thanksgiving. Our friends spent the next day with us, "to finish up the rice puddings," as Aunt Horton said, and then all returned to their homes. The next week Elizabeth returned to the seminary, and I again commenced going to school.

Winter passed by; and it was a cold, dreary New England winter, with a great depth of snow, that lay upon the ground until late in spring.

I took a violent cold, which I was not able to throw off, and which settled into a severe cough, so that I did not get rid of it until the warm weather of summer came; consequently, I did not enter the Young Ladies' Seminary until the fall term. Bell Jones, Laura Greenwood, Mary Osgood, and myself entered together, which made it very pleasant, as all others were strangers to us.

The school-building was quite imposing in its outward appearance, built of brick, three stories and basement in height, and proportionately large upon the ground, fronting the east, with north and south wings; at the front entrance was a spacious hall and corridors, leading entirely through the main building, and narrower ones through the two wings, at right angles from the main entrance.

The house was thronged during "opening day" with

scholars and their parents and friends who had brought them hither. We were assigned rooms in the third story, with windows looking toward the south, upon as beautiful a landscape as the eye ever beheld ; the broad river, flowing majestically through the meadows; the trees were putting on their beautiful autumn tints, and everything around seemed as though Nature's greatest artist had dipped his pencil in his most exquisite colors, and had painted in such numberless varieties of shades as to render the scenery beautiful beyond description.

Early the following morning the bell sounded, and, as by instinct, we quickly arose, and hastened our toilets, and, at the sound of the second bell, the girls all left their rooms, and were directed into the large dining-room, and, before sitting to the tables, we were addressed by the principal of the seminary, as follows:

"Young ladies, your parents have sent you to me to be instructed and fitted for usefulness in life ; and by my individual efforts, and by the aid of my assistants, I shall spare no labor nor pains to make you as proficient as possible in all the sciences to which you shall devote your attention. But remember the words of the old poet, 'Earn thy reward ; God gives naught to sloth,' and bear in mind that the few months or years you are to spend with me is precious time, and that if you neglect these golden opportunities and waste your time in idleness, you will have it to regret in after-life."

We then sat down to a breakfast of plain but substantial fare, and, after breakfast and worship, repaired to our rooms to await the call to examination, which was held during the day.

There were over three hundred scholars, and of that number there were about seventy new ones. I soon formed acquaintances, and many that afterward became very dear friends.

The first few weeks of our school passed off quietly, nothing of note occurring to disturb the equilibrium of our minds and interrupt our thoughts of home.

As many of the girls were comparative strangers to each other, a certain degree of reserve was manifested by nearly all, and those of us especially who had just entered the seminary were intent upon our studies (at least, it was so with me), that we might stand well in our recitations and thus command the respect of the lady principal and teachers.

Winter at last came upon us, and with it evening parties, public lectures, held in the town-hall, and an occasional sleigh-ride was enjoyed.

The principal of the seminary, Miss Haywood, was in appearance one of those precise, conservative ladies who feared to give expression, either by word or act, to the real sentiments of her soul, lest she would seem undignified and thereby fail to convey that impression of awe which ladies who occupy such positions seem to think is essential. The result was that, while all feared her, none loved her: consequently, there was no filial obedience. The teachers, on the whole, were genial and sympathetic, often engaging with the girls in their innocent evening sports.

Agreeable to promise when I left home, I wrote one letter each week to my parents, and as regularly received replies from them, all of which I have preserved with care, for the valuable lessons of instruction they contained, and the deep, parental solicitude manifested upon every page. And if young ladies could all realize fully the depth of paternal love, and the deep anxiety of parents for their welfare, I am sure there would be fewer erring ones than there are. And, exposed to temptations as I was while at the seminary, I very much fear that had it not been for those frequent missives of love from home, re-

plete with wisdom, I should have gone astray, or at least
so far neglected my opportunities as to have caused me
sincere regrets in after-life ; and, when hearing other girls
remark that they had not heard from home for several
weeks, I could but think that their parents either from igno-
rance neglected an important duty, or were wholly devoid
of that degree of solicitude which ought always to be ex-
ercised by parents for their children. And, being naturally
of a philosophical turn, I took pains to note the progress
of certain girls with whom I was the most familiar, and
I found it an invariable rule that those who lived the
nearest, in correspondence, thought, and affection, with
their friends at home, were the most proficient scholars.
I also soon learned another important fact in this connection, which was, that those girls who often received
letters from their parents received more attention than
others from the principal ; for the postman, who delivered
the letters to the seminary, was charged to deliver them
to no one but herself : thus she was aware of all the correspondence, and never, until she had inspected the en-
velopes, did she send them to the rooms where they
belonged.

With my close application to studies, frequent and
regular correspondence with my parents, occasional letters to and from my brothers and sisters and other friends,
my time was thoroughly occupied ; consequently, I saw
but little, comparatively, of Miss Haywood, at least saw
her but seldom out of school-hours, during the first two
months which I spent at the seminary.

One evening, late in the winter, I was sitting in my
room alone, reading over the second time a precious letter
received from my mother (my room-mate being at an
evening party, to which I was also invited), when I heard
a gentle rap at my door, and, on opening it, I quite unex-

4

pectedly met Miss Haywood. She came in and seated herself. I was so greatly surprised at this unusual occurrence that I knew not what to say. She seemed to observe my embarrassment, and at once handed me a letter, saying, "Aspasia, I have another letter from your father for you." I thanked her, and remarked that I was just reading over the second time my mother's last letter. She then inquired why I did not attend the party that evening, and if I did not receive an invitation. "Oh, yes," I replied; "I received a very polite invitation; but it was the day that I should hear from home, and I preferred to stay in my room and read and answer the letter; but as this letter did not come when I expected, I could enjoy myself no better than in reading over my mother's last letter." She remarked, "Your parents must indeed cherish for you the highest degree of affection, and I am sure it is fully reciprocated on your part; and I have become so impressed at the frequent correspondence between yourself and your parents, and also your rapid progress in your studies, that I am persuaded you will do credit to yourself, and honor your parents and this institution; and I have called upon you this evening, I presume unexpectedly to you, to assure you of my special regard; for 'virtue earns its own reward;' and if I can be of any special service to you at any time, you are at liberty to send for me or call at my room. And in your next letter to your parents give them my regards, and say to them that by their faithfulness to their daughter they have placed me under obligations."

She kissed me a good-night, and retired, and, for several moments, I sat as one that dreamed. I could hardly believe it was a reality that the august presence of the lady principal of the seminary had manifested herself in my room; but, dropping a book I held in my hand, I awoke from my reveries, and seizing my father's letter, which Miss Haywood had so kindly brought me, I tore open the envelope, and hastily read as follows:

"MY AFFECTIONATE DAUGHTER ASPASIA:—Your highly esteemed letter of the 25th ultimo reached us on the 27th, and would have been answered that same evening but for press of business, which absolutely prevented. Your mother and myself have read and re-read the letter, as we do all of your precious letters. Dear daughter, you cannot fully appreciate the real happiness you confer upon us by your frequent letters; and to know, as we do, that our dear child, away from home, in the company of so many young and lively ladies, and introduced to so many gay and lively scenes to which hitherto you were a stranger, is still so deeply attached to her parents as to neglect every other pleasure for the privilege of frequent correspondence, every line of which breathes forth the greatest depth of filial affection, is, I assure you, a consolation and pleasure that none but a parent can appreciate and understand. And, independent of the joy which it brings to us, we are glad to know that you value your privileges, and have fully resolved to improve every moment you are to spend at the seminary to become highly educated, and thus be prepared for usefulness in life, and enjoy the bliss of heaven in just that much greater degree; for I believe that saints in glory will immediately enter upon degrees graduated according to their intellectual attainments; and that is one reason—if not the reason—why our Lord seemed to place so much importance upon the cultivation of the talents he had given to men, and led him to utter the parable of the talents.

"You wrote that you were invited to an evening party on Tuesday. We suppose you will accept the invitation;

but, whether you do or not, we wish you to remember that your time is comparatively short at the seminary, and that, after you have completed your education, you will have the capacity to learn more from society in one week, or at least in one month, than you now can in an entire year. And your mother and I have concluded to take you and Elizabeth and spend your next summer's vacation at the sea-side. We can, therefore, only urge upon you, what we know you will perform,—viz., the closest attention to your studies.

"With a father's love,

"EDWARD HORTON."

I folded the letter, with my eyes nearly blinded with tears of gratitude and love, and, it being late, retired for the night.

# CHAPTER IV.

"When virtuous thoughts warm the celestial mind,
    With generous heat each sentiment's refined;
    Th' immortal perfumes breathing from the heart,
    With grateful odors sweeten every part.

"But when our vicious passions fire the soul,
    The clearest fountains grow corrupt and foul;
    The virgin springs, which should untainted flow,
    Run thick, and blacken all the stream below."

IT was a saying among the ancient Grecian philosophers that no master could be found that was qualified to
instruct others in virtue. One of them, referring to the
beauty and attractiveness of youth, by reason of dress
and perfumes, inquired of Socrates, "But as for you and
me, who are past the age, what ought we to possess?"
and received an answer replete with wisdom:—"Virtue
and honor."

As I peruse the pages of Grecian history, and study
the profound philosophy taught by the men of wisdom
and culture of that nation in that dark and dreary age, I
can but admire and venerate them; and if some of them
were not righteous before God, they come so very close to
it that I am unable to distinguish the difference between
them and Christians; for, surely, if Christians lived as
fully up to the light they enjoy as many of the ancient
Grecian philosophers did, we should witness a far greater
degree of true piety and godly sincerity evinced in their
daily life than we now do. And, while they lamented
that no man was capable of teaching virtue, we, who live

under a Christian dispensation, have One, the man Christ Jesus, who is able to teach his fellow-man virtue.

I was led to the foregoing reflections by a conversation I had with one of the girls at the seminary during my first year. Her name was Rose Blackwell; her parents resided in Boston, and were very wealthy, and, as I gathered from her in frequent conversations, she had (to use a homely phrase) "had her own way ever since she was born." When she was quite young, if she wished for anything, and was refused, all that was necessary on her part was to cry, and she was sure to get it. Of course she soon learned that she could be the master, or, rather, mistress, of any situation in which she might be placed, and, following an immutable law, as she grew older her self-will grew more stubborn, and her filial attachments weaker, until she had become so obdurate and willful that she was always unhappy, and a very disagreeable companion. She was very fond of dress, and her milliner's and mantua-maker's bills were enormous. But, to use her own language, "Law me! what do I care? father has plenty of money, and it can be appropriated to no better purpose." She had a great dislike to study, and could not endure quiet reflection. I have heard her say she would rather go deranged, and lose her reason entirely, than to be compelled to sit down alone and think. As may be inferred, she was exceedingly morose; and, notwithstanding all these disagreeable traits of character, she was very attractive to strangers, for Nature had endowed her with a good intellect, perfection of form and feature, added to which, her splendid dress made her the center of attraction among strangers wherever she went, all which was pleasing to her vanity and flattering to her pride, and, unconsciously to her, increased her haughtiness and self-will.

Although I never associated with Rose more than courtesy demanded, yet we had become pretty well acquainted; and I could not resist the conviction that, from some unexplainable cause, she had taken a great fancy to me.

It was not because I flattered her, or courted her company; for, while that was true of many in the seminary, it was not of me, for I never did either. I rarely, if ever, held conversation with her for five minutes at a time that I did not upbraid her for her evil deeds; and I never sought her society.

One Sabbath, being ill, I did not attend church; my room-mate did. Thus I was left alone. Soon after, all who were going to church had left the seminary, some one rapped loudly at my door. I at once opened it, feeling a little vexed that my solitude should be disturbed; and who should it be but Rose Blackwell? I invited her in and to a seat.

Being seated, she inquired, " Well, Aspasia, how happens it that you do not attend church to-day ?"

I replied that I felt quite ill, and therefore unable to go out. " But," said I, " why are not you at church ?"

" Well," said she, "that is one thing I have come to talk with you about; but, if you are too ill, I will return to my room and call upon you at another time."

I thought within myself, " Now, here is an opportunity to do good. God has kept me from church to give this young lady an opportunity, it may be, to unburden her soul to me, and possibly acknowledge her errors and ask for advice."

I therefore replied, that I was not so ill but that I should be pleased to converse with her if I could do her any good.

" Yes," said she, " there it is again. Do any good !

I never in my life saw a girl that was always so intent upon doing somebody some good as you are; but, to tell you the truth, I want to have a good long talk with you, whether it does either of us any good or not."

"Well," said I, "speak on. Unburden your soul, Rose, if you have anything to say; but, mind you, I want none of your nonsense."

"Nonsense!" said she. "What do you call nonsense?"

"I will tell you. There has scarcely been a conversation between us that you have not spoken ill of many of the girls in the seminary, and rarely, if ever, spoken well of one. And you have thrust upon me your skepticisms of religion, when you very well knew it was not only annoying to me, but you must have known it caused me pain. You have made light of religion, and ridiculed my professions. Now, all this is nonsense. You yourself do not believe you are right. You are dissatisfied with yourself. Your soul is not at rest. There is a disquietude which of itself renders you unhappy, and, unless you change your course, will end in your complete ruin."

"Well," said she, "it is unusual to preach a sermon without a text; but you have done it, sure."

"No," I replied, "for your everyday life, since you have been in the seminary, has been a living text to me, and I have longed for an opportunity to preach you this sermon, as you style it. Not that I have the least idea you will heed it, but to discharge my duty to you; for I should love to see you a better girl. And were you to put away your evil habits and thoughts, and change your whole course of life, with the wealth and influence you can command, your strong will and persistency of purpose, you can accomplish a vast amount of good, and also be respected and loved by every one; while now there are many weak-minded ones who flatter and fawn around you simply because of the elegance of your dress and the great wealth your father possesses. There are very few, if any, who sincerely love you, whose affection is so deep and lasting as that they would cling to you even though cold adversity should come upon you; and come it may, for aught you or I can tell; and should it come, you will then feel the need of true friendship."

To this she replied, " You are pretty severe with me. If I really thought I was as bad as you have represented, I should be driven to despair. I really wish I had not called on you. But, somehow, I fancied you were my real friend ; and you have conducted yourself in such an unostentatious manner and apparent consistency with your professions that, as you very well know, the entire school has come to respect and esteem you, myself among the rest."

To which I replied that I was not aware that I had merited any special respect; that from principle I meant to so conduct myself as to command at least an ordinary degree of respect from all my acquaintances ; and I assured her that my severe criticisms upon herself were not prompted by a desire to wound her feelings or render her unhappy, but solely because she possessed attributes of mind which, if rightly directed, would make her a loved and lovable lady.

"Well," said she, "if I am in so ill a state, you certainly ought to understand the remedy. What is your prescription ?"

" You must first subdue your stubborn will, and realize fully that other girls in the seminary possess equal rights with you in all respects ; that birth and wealth in reality have nothing at all to do in determining the status of a person in society, and that there is but one standard to measure people by, which is, intelligence and moral worth.

You must love to do good and hate to do evil; and, to understand what good and evil are, you must study the Bible attentively, for you can learn it nowhere else. And, so far as the fleeting pleasures of this life are concerned, you must bring yourself to feel and realize that all such is vanity; and, with your flatterers about you, and the evil influences to which you are constantly exposed, I can only warn you against them in the language of the old poet:

> "See, Vice, preventing every wish, appears
> To lead through down-hill paths and gay parterres
> Where Pleasure reigns; while Virtue, decent maid,
> Retires from view in yon sequester'd shade.
> Craggy and steep the way to her abodes;
> Fatigue and Pain, by order of the gods,
> Stern sentry keep. But if nor pain nor toil
> Can check the generous ardor of thy soul,
> Exert thy powers, nor doubt thy labor's meed.
> Conquest and joy shall crown the glorious deed."

She sat for a moment in silence. At last she spoke.

"You reason like a philosopher; and I confess I never before received so severe a lesson; and I did not know I was so bad and unlovable, neither was I aware that my acquaintances thought me so. I supposed that in order to be admired I must be gay and thoughtless, and that to command respect I must assume an air of haughtiness; but, if your philosophy is correct, it teaches directly the reverse."

"Yes," I replied, "it is true; and you will yet acknowledge it to me; for I am fully convinced that you are dissatisfied with your course of life, have promised yourself that, if you could obtain aid and sympathy from others, you would amend your ways; and I assure you I will aid you with all my power. You shall have my warmest sympathy; and I believe I do but express the feelings of very many of the young ladies in the seminary."

To which she replied, "You surprise me. You could not have read my thoughts more correctly had they been recorded in a book; I thank you most sincerely for this interview, and shall ponder upon what you have said, and assure you I take it kindly, for I know it has been spoken in the spirit of love; I beg the privilege of another interview at your future convenience."

I replied that I should be pleased to see her at my room at her convenience. By this time the girls were returning from church, she retired to her room, and I put up a silent prayer to Jesus that he would send his guardian angel to watch over her and shield her from temptation, that the Holy Spirit would strengthen her resolutions, show her clearly her duty, and give her strength to perform it.

It may seem strange that in this my first conversation I did not endeavor to impress more forcibly upon her the absolute necessity of repentance of sins and confession before God But my reason was, that, knowing as I did her bitter hostility to religion, had I taken that course at the first I should have repelled her, and probably been unable to regain her confidence; whereas, as subsequent events have proven, by the wisdom given me of God, I did right; for, without detailing subsequent conversations (and we had many, and very happy ones), I will simply add that Rose became a devoted Christian, and that through her efforts her parents were both converted. She married a wealthy merchant, who was an active Christian; and, her parents both dying at about the same time, she became sole heiress to her father's estate, the entire amount of which she appropriated to the service of her Lord and

Saviour  Thus she became the almoner of God's bounty, to feed the hungry and clothe the naked ; and in after-years, as the sequel will prove, I myself, in poverty, was made the recipient of bounties most generously bestowed, verifying the truth of Scripture, " Cast thy bread upon the waters, and thou shalt find it again after many days."

Thus the few crumbs of truth that I was permitted to sow in her heart did indeed, by the grace of God, ripen into a glorious harvest.

# CHAPTER V.

SPRING came, and with it all nature awoke from the cold sleep of winter. The beautiful bluebirds were the early messengers from a southern clime to announce that spring-time had come. Soon following them, the robin-redbreast sent up his notes of joy, that the season had permitted the return of himself and mate to the happy home he had enjoyed the past season, and where they reared their little family of warblers.

The grass grew green in the meadows. The herds that had been confined within the yards or stalls, as within prison-walls, during a long and cold winter, were now let loose in the pastures, and, by awkward antics, gave expression to their joy at being free again. The orchards, ornamental trees, and forests were being again clothed with luxuriant foliage, all typical of the spring-time of life, when hope is buoyant, the affections fervent, the soul alive with energy, and the physical system full of life and vigor.

As the warm weather came on, I began to count the days that intervened before the close of the term and my return home; for of all places on earth there was to me no such place as home,—"the dear old home." And now, in after-years, while meditating upon my childhood days, with vivid recollections home scenes come fresh to my mind, and I almost wish I were a girl again.

5 ( 49 )

" When I long for sainted memories,
    Like angel troops they come,
If I fold my hands and ponder
    On the dear old home;
To that sweet spot forever,
    As to some hallowed dome,
Life's pilgrim bends his vision
    To his dear old home.

" A father sat, how proudly then,
    By that dear hearthstone's ray,
And told his children stories
    Of his early manhood's day;
And one soft eye was beaming,
    From child to child 'twould roam;
Thus a mother counts her treasures
    In the dear old home.

" The birthday gifts and festivals,
    The blended vesper hymn,
Some dear ones, who were swelling it,
    Are with the seraphim.
The fond ' good-nights,' at bedtime,
    How quiet sleep would come
And fold us all together,
    In the dear old home.

" Like a wreath of scented flowerets,
    Close intertwined each heart,
But time and change in concert
    Have blown the wreath apart;
But sainted, sainted memories,
    Like angels ever come,
If I fold my arms and ponder
    On the dear old home."

At last the term closed, and that was a lively day at
the seminary. Such leave-takings! for while all longed
to be freed from the monotony of school life, and for

home, still attachments had been formed which caused deep regrets at the final parting.

My father came for me in his carriage. I saw him coming up the road, and ran to meet him. I could not wait until he should reach the house; he seemed dearer to me than ever.

My trunk was packed all ready to leave on his arrival, so that he was detained but a few moments, just long enough for the "hired man" to place it in the carriage; while I was putting on my things, he was expressing his gratitude to Miss Haywood for her kindnesses to his daughter, assuring her of his appreciation for all the special favors so generously granted, and that he hoped for an opportunity to reciprocate, assuring her that, if life and health were spared, I should return to the seminary at the commencement of the fall term, and complete my education under her care.

We were soon seated in the carriage, and rapidly journeying toward home, where we arrived in due time, and were greeted by mother, brothers, and sisters, as none but a loved one could be; in turn, I shed tears of joy upon meeting the dear ones at home once more; even old Rover, although growing aged and indolent, manifested all the emotions of joy the poor brute was capable of.

All those young ladies who have spent their first years away from home, and at a boarding-school, will appreciate my feelings at this time.

My father hastened with his work, that we might all enjoy the promised journey and spend a season at the sea-side; and, in the mean time, I occupied myself by assisting in the house-work, visiting at sister Kate's, calling upon and entertaining friends. In a few weeks my father gave brother William such advice and directions concerning the management of affairs, that he could leave the business with him, and we prepared for the journey.

Elizabeth determined to be fashionable, and "create a sensation" (as she laughingly said), "at least among the baggage-men, if nowhere else," and persuaded father to purchase a Saratoga trunk of the largest size manufactured, and was anxious I should also have one, but I preferred my little old trunk. Upon packing, however, she soon found she had quarters to let, for, with our views of economy, one such was sufficient for the entire family; so it was finally concluded that mother, sister, and myself would enter into joint occupancy of "the trunk," and father could take a satchel. This pleased him, because he could carry it, and then have but one piece of baggage to look after, and that one so enormously large, there was no more danger of losing it than there would be of losing an ordinary-sized story-and-a-half dwelling.

Mother suggested that father have his name painted on each end; but this was objected to. There was an old sign painted in large Roman letters, in black, upon white ground, "G. Horton." This sign had been lying in the garret for many years, it being one that my father had on his store years previous. William suggested that it be nailed on Elizabeth's trunk. This was objected to, lest some burglar, mistaking it for a dry-goods or millinery store, might possibly break in, and, by his robberies, seriously embarrass us. It was finally concluded to place a card on each end with father's name; and, thus equipped and furnished, we started on our summer tour. Upon getting "the trunk" checked at the depot, the agent, who was well acquainted with father, and was, withal, a genial, kind-hearted, and obliging gentleman, looked with astonishment at our baggage; and said he, "Mr. Horton, we shall have to charge you two dollars extra for the trunk." And in vain did my father attempt to convince him that that was most decidedly against public policy; that there were four of us, and only one trunk. "True," he said, "but it is a very large one, and I would handle six common-sized trunks in preference to one of those things." Father paid him two dollars extra, and took his check, and we were soon off for Albany. Nothing of note occurred on the way. The cars did not fly the track; there were no broken rails or drunken engineers; and, I think, but one young man was killed by the train that day, which was considered by the train-men of little importance. "He was only a track laborer," the conductor said. This expression sent a thrill of horror through my soul, and I repeated it, "Only a track laborer." But was he not a man? Perhaps he had a mother, wife, or children, that were the sharers of his daily earnings, and who would mourn and lament his death and their irreparable loss.

Arriving at Albany, father handed his check to the omnibus agent in the cars, and designated his hotel; and, soon after being shown to our rooms, a porter handed a note to father, which he found, on opening, was a charge of one dollar for handling extra baggage. He was truly indignant, and went directly to the office to explain, and stated that there were four of us and but one trunk. But the clerk could not afford him any assistance, and he paid it and returned to his room. By this time, Elizabeth was beginning to dislike the sensation her trunk was creating; though but little was said; it was all for fashion. Some people seem to enjoy disappointments, useless expense, and great annoyances, if it is in the cause of fashion; but it didn't sit well upon any one of us.

We spent a few days very pleasantly in Albany, visiting friends and seeing the city, and took the cars for

Montreal. And this time, to avoid the annoyance, father handed the porter a dollar extra to put the trunk on board the cars; but, when he came to procure his check, he had another extra baggage bill to pay. Were it not that father was an even-tempered, philosophical sort of a man, I am sure he would have lost his patience with Elizabeth for urging its purchase; but not a murmur escaped his lips.

Arriving at Montreal, and ever after on the journey, father inquired of each porter and baggage-man who handled "the trunk," "How much charge for extra baggage?" and immediately paid their price.

In due time we left Montreal for "the States," again by rail, and on our way were so unfortunate, and yet fortunate, as to encounter an accident.

My father always, if possible, avoided either the first or the last car in a train if there were more than two; for, he said, the first was the most liable to an accident which might happen to the engine, and the last was liable to be thrown from the track by rapidly turning the curves; but when we arrived at the depot it was late, and we took seats in the first car we reached, which was the rear one in the train. After we had traveled a couple of hours or so, while running rapidly on a down grade, following the zigzag course of a mountain brook, and while swiftly rounding a curve, the last car (in which we were riding) was whirled off the track, and rolled completely over down the hill, and came near landing us all in the brook. Such a jumbled-up mess as we were! The car was filled with passengers, and in an instant, as it were, we were hurled over the embankment, and rattled against the sides, top, and bottom (as one man said), "like cobs in a corn-sheller." I felt a good deal as the Irishman did, who was accidentally knocked down. Some one asked if he was dead. "No, indade," said he, "I'm not dead, but spacheless."

The car finally landed on its side. The train was stopped as soon as possible, and ran back to us, the passengers all left the other cars in haste, to render those in ours assistance. All were taken or helped out in a few moments. Of course the car was badly broken, and although a majority of the passengers escaped in a miraculous manner from receiving serious injuries, yet many were injured, and some, it was feared, fatally. Thanks to a kind Providence (but no thanks to the engineer or conductor), our party escaped comparatively uninjured. Mother and Elizabeth sustained slight bruises only. But the groans of those who were seriously hurt were indeed painful. Yet, amid the horrors of the catastrophe, there were many ludicrous scenes; one in particular. A gentleman, apparently about fifty years of age, with his wife and two grandchildren, occupied the two seats back of me, and I could not avoid observing their movements on the journey; for although the children were old enough to have put up with regular meals, yet at every station the woman would trot her husband out with a white glass bottle for milk and a handful of eatables for the darlings. And when the stations were frequent, he would object; but one snappish word, and her sarcastic look, was sufficient: he went, and thus revealed the fact that he had surrendered all his manhood (if he ever had any) to a woman wholly void of culture and destitute of grace.

In freeing the passengers from the debris that was piled over and about them, this woman was taken out, considerably scared, but not much "hurt." Her first inquiry was for "John" (her husband). She was informed he had not yet been found. "Well," said she, "I suppose he's dead, poor soul; nobody is to blame but he; I never should have come but for him. I suppose the bottle is broke, too; that's one my mother gave me, and I set store by it." Her husband seemed first in her mind, because he was a thing of service to her; the bottle next, because it was an heirloom.

The wounded were quickly put on board the train, and taken to the nearest station and cared for in a manner so well understood by railroad officials.

It is really surprising to see how the apprehension of heavy damages operates to develop congeniality and sympathetic love. Such spontaneous gushes of tender-heartedness are truly affecting. The love of money, or, having it, the fear of losing, goes far toward smoothing down the rough edges of a character otherwise morose and unapproachable; and my experience teaches me that there are a great many persons of this character in every community. None but motives of supreme selfishness can ever draw from them expressions of sympathy. Their heart is like an iceberg, and, as we approach them, an icy chilliness comes over us. And what a relief and pleasure it is to change the society of such for those whose every word and look is an expression of sympathy and love, and, whatever the circumstances or position in life of the suffering ones, their hearts are ever open to permit the ready exercise of tender emotions, which at once and always are manifested by good deeds!

As soon as the injured passengers were discharged from the cars, at the nearest station from the place where the accident occurred, the train again started on its trip, and we were whirled along at a furious rate (yet without further accident) to the end of our journey, arriving at our hotel at ———— in the evening, dusty and fatigued. Father at once ordered supper of sea diet. And such a supper! Roast mackerel, baked salmon, clams, whortleberries, and fruits in abundance; and, as we were greatly fatigued and hungry withal, we were as voracious as an army of bashiquas, and I thought I never tasted anything half so rich; but, after spending a few days there, and becoming accustomed to this diet, I found it like other pleasures or blessings of life, that we are apt to lose our appreciation of them by constant enjoyment.

We spent several weeks at this place, and the most of the time the weather was delightful : there were a great many visitors at this sea-side town, and we formed many agreeable and profitable acquaintances. We occupied our time in sea-bathing, fishing, strolling over the hills, and in entertaining and being entertained by guests of the various hotels and a few citizens of the town with whom we formed acquaintance.

It was amusing to one who could occupy a private box as I did, and, with a quizzing-glass, have full opportunity to criticise those who were playing upon the stage of fashion, to note the different temperaments, dispositions, habits of thought, rule of life, judgment, and tastes for dress.

There was the honest, unassuming, prudent gentleman and lady, of which my father and mother were fit representatives. With all such (and there were many) we enjoyed ourselves greatly. They were uniformly intelligent and communicative, and conversation with them was both pleasant and profitable. This class made no show, and created no sensation (as it is usually termed): still, they commanded and received great respect.

There was another class, who were originally very poor, but, by energy and a favorable turn of Fortune's wheel, had become wealthy. Many such were affable and unassuming; but, to use a homely expression, the shoddy would stick out, in the mother and daughters especially; and such gewgaws as they would pile on, without any taste or judgment, but wholly ignoring all chaste and refined rules of dress by the piling on of trinkets! One would suppose that the height of their ambition was simply to outshine some one, forgetting that it is the fixed stars which shine with the greatest brilliancy and whose scintillations are the most observed. Occasionally one of those flirting little meteors will pass over the glass of the astronomer; but it does not attract his attention, nor cause him to withdraw his gaze from those greater and more luminous orbs.

There was still another class of gentlemen and ladies, of great wealth, who inherited fortunes, and have, notwithstanding their extravagances, continued to increase those fortunes. These were generally good-natured people, quick of apprehension, at the same time courteous and polite, but careful not to admit within the inner circle of their acquaintances any but those who were rich in ancestral estates. These were the remnants of the old-school aristocracy, which, I am pleased to know, is fast dying out in this country.

There was still another class of wealthy people, who were ignorant and selfish; who never gave to charity, never paid the price asked for any article, and, unless they could hire a carriage for less than others cheerfully paid, would go to the beach on foot. They seemed willing to suffer any amount of inconvenience to gratify their avarice. They all, parents and children, seemed to have been most thoroughly educated in this school. They were despised and shunned by all except congenial spirits, and even between them there was really no respect.

Then there was the flirt and her fop, come down from the city to view the countraw. It was impossible to judge correctly of the pecuniary standing of this class, but, from their conversation and manners, I judged they were poor, and always had been, and were sure to remain so, for, without exception, they were illiterate and shallow-brained. The simple fact that they were poor in this world's goods was not to their discredit; far from that; but being so, and attempting to palm themselves off upon strangers as persons of wealth and character, is like dealing in counterfeit three-cent currency: if it is discovered on your hands, the loss is so trifling that the transaction passes without a thought or reflection. So with this last class of persons referred to. They simply attract the same attention that counterfeit currency does, and they are as readily detected and as readily pass out of use.

Then there was the morose old bachelor, wrapped up in his selfishness. He rode every day alone in the best carriage the livery afforded; seemed to spend money freely, and, in his way, I have no doubt, enjoyed life. But it's an odd way. With him society was nothing only so far as it contributed to his selfish enjoyments. Such men remind me of an occasional tree, standing solitary and alone in the midst of one of the vast prairies of the West; all about and beneath it was dry and barren, yet there it stood, neglected and alone. Contrast this with the trees in the forest, nursery, or orchard : clustering together, they spread their luxuriant foliage to catch the dews of the night, pouring the same upon the tender herb beneath and around them, and, by their life-giving principles, the tender plants spring up all about them, and under their shade, either to be transplanted in some beautiful garden, or take the place of the original tree when it decays.

Then there were gentlemen and ladies who belonged to the genuine aristocracy ; I mean an aristocracy of worth, where the goddess of Virtue reigns; whose hearts are full of love; who are religious from principle, and are in all things what they profess. True, there are men and women of this class of different temperaments; some so sanguine, and a little nervous withal, that they are very frequently misjudged by those of an opposite temperament, and *vice versa.* Yet carefully keep watch of them all, and we discover that, without ostentation, they do and perform those duties which none but the Christian does. We hear them in their closets, " O Lord, subdue my stubborn will," " Increase my faith," " Heal all my backslidings, and forgive all my sins." And, even though at the sea-side for pleasure, we find them at the weekly prayermeetings of the village church, encouraging the few faithful ones in their Christian duties, both by precept and example.

Such, and even a still greater variety of characters, did we find and meet with while at the sea-side; and the "lessons in life" which I read then and there have been of great service to me.

I cannot close my notes upon this sea-side visit without detailing a conversation I had with a gentleman and two ladies, who called at our rooms the last Wednesday evening we were there. All had gone to the prayer-meeting but myself. Feeling slightly ill, I remained at home; and Mr. Goodspeed and the two Miss Graves called to spend the evening. They were well-educated people, affable and kind-hearted, but were mere moralists; did not believe in the divinity of Christ.

On inquiring for my sister Elizabeth, and being informed that she, with my parents, had gone to the prayer-meeting, and that I was prevented only by slight indisposition, Mr. Goodspeed remarked, " I had formed an exalted opinion of yourself and sister, and did not suppose you were so foolish as to deprive yourselves of the pleasures of life by doing penance."

"Sir," said I, "although I think I enjoy life as heartily as any person, still my happiest moments are those when brought nearest my Saviour; and frequently I get strayed so far away from him, while running after the glittering toys of earth, that I need to be brought into close fellow-ship with Christians, and feel the influence of their hearts (as they are manifested in love, faith, and repentance) upon my own, to quicken me to duty, and cause me to anchor still stronger than ever to Jesus, the rock of my salvation."

"Well," said one of the ladies, "since your parents and sister are at the prayer-meeting, and religion seems to be a favorite theme with you, we should be pleased to hear your views upon two or three points that we think call for a little explanation :

"First. How can God consistently hold the heathen responsible for not serving him, without ever providing them with a written religion and informing them of Jesus Christ, their Saviour, or, at least, whom you or-thodox call a Saviour ?

"Second. Where is the fairness in God's withholding his Saviour from men for four thousand years, and still sending them by millions down to hell (as you profess to believe) for being sinners?

"Third. If God is all-powerful, how does it happen that the devil has so many more devotees than God? for certainly, if the world comes to an end so soon as is preached, according to your theory the devil will have much the largest company, and the all-powerful and strongest ought to meet with the greatest success.

"I have asked these questions often, and have never yet received a satisfactory answer."

I replied that I felt a little delicacy at attempting to answer questions covering such broad grounds and involving theological truths of so momentous importance; yet, presuming they would not expect a full discussion of all the points involved, I would proceed to answer in as concise a manner as possible.

"And, first, God was under no obligation to man, in any sense of that term. He first created him perfectly pure and holy as one of the angels before his throne. At the same time he gave him, as one of the necessary elements of a moral being, free agency, or the exercise of his own will. He placed him upon this earthly paradise, for the whole earth before the fall was a paradise, when fitted for the abode of man, God's representative on earth ('God looked upon it and saw that it was good'), and surrounded him with everything that was beautiful and calculated to stimulate the holiest emotions of his soul. But, alas! he sinned, and the earth was cursed on account of that sin; and as sin had come into the world, so came death; for God had forewarned the man that if he sinned against him he should surely die,—having especial reference to the death of the body, from which there can be no escape; for God, who is the author of all law, had established a law that a single transgression on the part of Adam, man's first representative on earth, should render the physical system mortal and subject to disease, pain, and death; and the transgression also brought upon the soul of the transgressor eternal death. In the economy of God's grace, such effects of the fall could not be entailed upon men of succeeding ages. Hence it was early said, 'The wicked shall die for his own sins;' 'The soul that sinneth, it shall die.' In view of this, God at once directed Adam to seek repentance for his sin, and to offer a sacrifice typical of the great sac-

rifice prepared for men after they had had sufficient time
to test their own vain philosophies and theories. So here,
at the very outset, God established his religion, and made
the first man, a converted sinner, a preacher; and he had
many eminent preachers all the way down to the time of
the flood. Everything was done that could consistently
be, by God, to bring men to love and obey him. But
no: they chose their own wicked ways; and even the de-
scendants of Noah, immediately after leaving the ark,
having been preserved from destruction in that miraculous manner, became great idolaters, and that, too, while
their father was yet a preacher of righteousness and men
were but few upon the earth. God then commenced sending his prophets as preachers, as he does nowadays, among
the people to preach to them; and the burden of all the
preaching, from Adam to Christ, was repentance and
faith on the Lord God, who was to come and offer himself a sacrifice to answer the demands of justice, in order
that God might pardon the sinner. And the people in
all those ages were enjoined to offer a sin-offering of the
blood of animals, as typical of Christ's great sacrifice that
was to be made. The only difference between the doctrines taught then and since Jesus came, are, that since
Christ died, repentance for sins and faith in a crucified
and risen Saviour are preached now. Then, where is
the injustice of God? He had done all he could, consistent with man's free agency, to flood the world with
the saving light of truth, but men were too obdurate to
receive it, and hence the condemnation has been the portion of a vast majority of all who have lived on the
earth,—not because God desired it, or withheld any
means or influences which he could consistently bestow
or bring to bear upon men, but wholly of their own
choosing. From Adam to Noah, and from Noah to Moses,

and from Moses to Christ, in all ages, men of superior talents, and eminent for their piety, of their own choice became preachers of righteousness and missionaries among the different nations; and we find these men were not confined to any one tribe or nation. For instance, we find Job, of the land of Uz, one of God's most perfect servants, a man of great wealth and commanding position, so wealthy, so noble, and so devoted to God, that God himself said of him that there was none like him on the· face of the whole earth. And from the fact that so renowned and wealthy a man as Job was a servant of God, we may presume there were many thousands of his people who were also righteous before God. Also the visit of the three Edomite princes, friends of Job, to condole with him in his deep affliction, and the language used by them makes it evident that they were reared under religious influences; and from the high character, standing, and great wealth of Job, we are led to the conclusion that his friends were of royal blood; therefore, religiously, as well as politically, they were representative men of the nation.

"Again, Melchizedek, one of the ancient kings, cotemporary with Abraham, yet, without doubt, possessing greater wealth and influence, was also a priest of God, as well as a king of great power and influence. Hence I conclude that his subjects must have been religious.

"Again, as we peruse the pages of ancient history, we are forced to the conclusion that Plato and very many of those old sages lived as near to God as the dim light of nature would guide them, and that Socrates died a martyr to the eternal principles of virtue and religion.

"And so soon as the Holy Spirit, by the vision, had removed the bigotry from the mind of the Apostle Peter, he made the astounding announcement 'that in every nation he that feareth God and worketh righteousness is accepted with him;' and this is in harmony with the declaration that 'the heathen are without excuse.'

"In answer to your third interrogatory, although it may be true that more souls have perished than have been saved, this will not be the final result; for 'the kingdoms of this world shall become the kingdoms of our Lord and of his Christ, and he shall reign for ever and ever;' and at the announcement the elders before the throne of God 'fell upon their faces, saying, We give thee thanks, O Lord God Almighty, which art, and wast, and art to come, because thou hast taken to thee thy great power, and hast reigned.' And it is added by the revelator, 'And the nations were angry, . . . . . and shouldest destroy them which destroy the earth.' By this latter clause I understand that, at the commencement of Christ's millennial reign, those nations and peoples who have persisted in opposing the religion of Jesus will be angry at the rapid success of Christianity, and that the Spirit of God will destroy the influences of Satan and his spirits who destroy the earth; for sin not only destroys the soul, but also the earth, for before sin entered into the world the earth brought forth of its own seed everything that was good, and only good.

"And as to the world coming to an end soon, I am aware that many have preached that the 'end of all things is at hand.' And so it is with many a person and people, as it was with the Jewish nation at the time those memorable words were uttered. But it is revealed to us that before the end of the world Christ shall reign on earth a thousand years. By this we are not to understand ten hundred of our years; for 'a thousand years is with the Lord as one day, and one day as a thousand years.' And, in the fulfillment of prophecy, this is the invariable rule for measuring God's time. So it was in the creation. Hence I believe that Christ is to reign supreme in the hearts of men on earth during three hundred and sixty-five thousand of our years; and, owing to this peaceful and happy condition of society throughout the world, deaths by disease will be less frequent, and never occur by violence. Consequently, the inhabitants of earth will be multiplied to thousands of millions, until the multitudes who shall worship Jesus shall be so great that no man nor angel can number them. And thus, at the day of judgment, those who shall go away with Satan to everlasting punishment shall be as a drop of water to an ocean, when compared with those who shall partake of Christ's kingdom and reign as kings and priests with him forever "

" Well," said the lady who propounded the interrogatories, " your answers and explanations are exceedingly interesting, and are new to us; and I confess that never before have these points been satisfactorily explained, and we cannot gainsay your arguments."

As the evening was far spent, they departed, and soon after my parents and sister returned from the meeting, and after our evening oblation we all retired for the night.

The next day we were taking leave of friends and packing " the trunk," preparatory for our departure for home, whither we reached that same week.

Thus ended our sea-side visit; and it was not without its beneficial effects upon our physical health; and we trust that we gained in knowledge and in religious growth, and that we were able also to impart blessings to others.

# CHAPTER VI.

"How swiftly glide life's transient scenes away!
Like vernal leaves, men flourish and decay.
Thus sung, in days of yore, the Chian bard;
This maxim all have heard, but none regard.
None keep in mind this solitary truth,
Hope still survives, that flatters us in youth.
What fruitless schemes amuse our blooming years!
The man in health nor age nor sickness fears;
Nay, youth's and life's contracted space forgot,
Scarce thinks that death will ever be his lot.
But thou thy mind's fair bias still obey,
Nor from the paths of virtue ever stray."

Soon after reaching home from my sea-side visit, I commenced preparations for my return to the seminary.

I entered at the commencement of the fall term; and many were the happy greetings as the young ladies assembled in the large hall of the building on that opening day.

One of the first to greet me on my return was Rose Blackwell; and I saw at a glance there had been a radical change in her, and it was so patent as to be the subject of general remark.

During this my second year in the seminary I visited in the neighborhood but little, devoting myself assiduously to my studies. Nothing of special interest transpired, and at the close of the spring term I again returned home,—but, alas! not to enjoy the pleasures of home, as formerly.

My mother (God bless her memory!) was taken ill

with a bilious attack just before I reached home.  Dr.
Woodman was called, and, on seeing her, "thought he
would be able to break up the fever," and "that she
would soon be about again."  But it was not so.  The
disease had gotten fast hold of her, and, having a strong
constitution, all the energies of her system volunteered
their aid in endeavoring to throw off the disease, and
thus the fever increased ; and, when I arrived at home,
she was so ill that she was obliged to have watchers by
her bedside constantly.

I had been at home but a few days when the doctor
informed my father that he feared mother would not recover.  It fell like the shock of an earthquake upon my
father.  For thirty-one years had my parents lived together
most happily, and their souls were knit together as the
soul of one.  They loved each other with a love as enduring as life; and their children loved them quite as ardently.

As soon as the doctor left, father called together all the
family, consisting of brother William, Kate, Elizabeth, and
myself, and informed us of the sad intelligence.  And, oh,
what sadness came over us!  And, amid our sobs and tears,
we knelt, and father prayed most fervently that, if it were
possible, this cup of affliction might pass from us ; nevertheless, if it was God's will that our dear mother should
be taken from us, we might have grace to bear up under
the great affliction.  After drying our tears, that we might
not needlessly excite mother, we all repaired to her room
and gathered about her bed.  She understood the meaning of it perfectly ; and, taking father's hand, she said,
" My dear husband and children, you think I am about to
die : I am also aware that I have but a few days at the
longest, and perhaps a few hours, to live with you here.
But, although my body will die, and you will bury it out
of your sight, my soul will put on newness of life.

" Oh, my dear husband and children, although it is trying for us to part as we are about to, yet how glorious to know that we are all Christians; that we are to meet again in that bright world beyond the flood, where Jesus is; that we shall all be permitted to join in praising our Redeemer forever; there shall be no sin, sickness, sorrow, or death! Methinks I hear the angels singing for joy that I am so soon to be welcomed into that blissful abode.

> " ' I would not live alway, I ask not to stay
> Where storm after storm rises dark o'er the way.' "

My mother seemed perfectly calm during all this time, while we were all overwhelmed with grief. She requested father to pray that we might all be strengthened to endure the trial, and that Jesus would manifest himself especially to her, and that he would go down into the dark waters with her, and bear her safely above them, and land her on the shores of that beautiful country that needs neither the light of the sun nor of the moon; "for the glory of God will lighten it, and the Lamb is the light thereof."

Word was sent that day by post to John and James, and they arrived the next day; and there was not a moment that some of us were not by our dear mother's bedside; and, oh, such joy as was manifested in her every look and word! For, while it pained her to leave her loved ones behind, still, she longed to be with her Saviour. Then it was that I realized the force of those words, " Let me die the death of the righteous, and let my last end be like his."

Mr. Shaw spent nearly all the time at our house during the last few days of mother's sickness. She died on Saturday morning. Many of the neighbors were in and about the house at the time; and, oh, what floods of grief were there poured forth!

Soon after her death, Deacon Jones requested of father that the corpse might be taken to the church for the funeral services on the Sabbath; for the whole townspeople would feel her loss deeply, and would wish to attend the funeral and take the last look of one so highly respected and loved.

To this father consented; and Mr. Shaw preached the funeral sermon, based upon the following texts of Scripture:

"Behold, he taketh away. Who can hinder him? who will say unto him, What doest thou?" "If a man die, shall he live again?"

I will not undertake to give a synopsis of the discourse; for I was so filled with grief that I could remember but portions of it.

Upon returning home that day, after we had laid the body of our dear mother in the grave and buried it out of sight forever, we felt lonely and sad, and we all gathered about our father, and said to him, "Now our dear mother has gone to heaven, and there is none to divide with you your children's love, and we now pledge you our sincerest affection, doubly increased for you, our dear father and only parent." And we all fell upon his neck and kissed him.

During the summer which followed, the superintendence of the affairs of the house devolved upon sister Elizabeth and myself; and at the commencement of the fall term I again entered the seminary. This being my last year, I applied myself to my studies, if possible, with greater diligence than previously; and the death of my dear mother rendered me lonely, and at times given to melancholy, which was increased in consequence of the constant tax upon my mental faculties.

Miss Haywood, observing this, took the very wise pre-caution to divert my mind as much as possible, and insisted that I should cultivate the mirthful element of my nature, and thus counteract the deleterious effects of my deep affliction and close application to books; for which I have often felt grateful, for I am persuaded that had I continued in the same frame of mind long in which I was when I entered upon that term, I should have early followed my mother to the spirit-world.

A short time after the commencement, I received a letter from Rose Blackwell, conveying the very pleasing intelligence that she was about to be married, and, consequently, should not return to the seminary as she expected, also sending a very polite invitation to me to attend her wedding. I at once wrote my father to learn his wish concerning it, and received his hearty consent.

I then wrote to Rose that, by and with the consent of my father, and most happily to myself, I accepted her invitation, and should leave for Boston on the morning of the day previous to the wedding. At the same time, I informed her of my mother's death.

At the appointed time I took the morning train for Boston to attend the wedding, arriving there at four o'clock P.M. Was met at the depot by Rose in her father's splendid carriage, and we were driven to her father's house, where I was as warmly welcomed as though I were one of their own children; and when Rose introduced me to her mother as her dear friend Miss Horton, said Mrs. Blackwell, "Pardon me, Miss Horton; please allow me to call you by your Christian name, Aspasia; for husband and myself could not love you more tenderly were you our own dear child, for your great kindness to Rose, and the immense good you have done us through your influence upon her."

Of course I consented, and remarked that, if I had been the humble instrument of good to them, she must give God the glory, it was all his; and I thanked her kindly for her generous expressions of love, assuring her that it was fully reciprocated. I also said that my state of mind had been such, owing to close attention to my studies, and the deep affliction I was called to endure, that I felt as though I needed a change for a day or two at least; but, after all, I should not have accepted a like invitation from any other friend. To this she replied that Rose had given her the painful news of my mother's death, and that, while it was sad to think of, and an irreparable loss, still we should receive it as an admonition, "Be ye also ready."

Soon Rose and I were left by ourselves in the drawing-room, and said I, "Rose, now tell me all about the gentleman you are to marry, who and what he is, and how you happen to be married just now."

"Well," said she, "last summer I went with my parents to the sea-side to spend the season. I met there very many of my former gay companions, and they endeavored to lead me off into all sorts of frivolities; but, seeing I was not thus inclined, they abandoned me wholly, and for several days my only society (and it was that which I especially desired) was that of my parents. They felt very unpleasantly about it; but I remarked that it was only for a short season, and the associations of such were really of no practical benefit to any one.

"There was a gentleman stopping at the same hotel with us, of courteous bearing, apparently a man of wealth and refinement, and very fine-looking also, yet he never seemed to seek or relish the society of the gay and thoughtless. My father formed his acquaintance in a political discussion, which was participated in by several, and father

was so favorably impressed with him that he invited him
to call on us, which he did on the next day. At his first
visit, we were all pleased with his appearance; as he
left, I ventured to accompany him to the door, and gave
him a polite invitation to repeat his visit, and to come
as frequently as agreeable to himself, and that, too,
without the least formality. And he availed himself of
my invitation to the fullest extent; for he called morning,
noon, and evening, at any and all times in the day. We
walked together and rode together, and both say we never
enjoyed ourselves so well as then. The result was, he
asked me to marry him; and, as I had anticipated him,
and obtained consent of my parents in advance, I replied
at once, and without the slightest hesitation, that I would,
with all my heart.

"Now as to who and what he is. He is George Shepherd, a wholesale dry-goods merchant on Milk Street,
in this city, and is a deacon in the —————— Church, and,
although young (twenty-eight years of age), he is very
wealthy. A large fortune was left him by an uncle, who
amassed wealth in the East India trade, and he has been
constantly adding to it. His habits of prudence and
economy have enabled him to give large sums for charitable purposes without impairing his necessary capital in
trade; and he says he believes 'it is more blessed to
give than to receive,' and that he has never felt so well
satisfied with himself as when he has just been called
upon to contribute to some charitable object. You shall
have an introduction to him this evening, as he will be
here."

Evening came, and Mr. Shepherd called, as was expected; and he proved in appearance just what my mind
had fancied; a little above the medium height, spare-
built, a noble countenance, genial and yet commanding

in his appearance, a quick, penetrating look, and a physiognomy which indicated a sagacity of judgment, generosity, reverence, and deep-toned sympathy; and, altogether, he was at sight my beau ideal of a man, and, upon acquaintance, I found him very agreeable in conversation, intelligent and communicative, without reserve or affectation.

Toward the close of the evening, after we had become somewhat familiar, he inquired why I was not looking up a husband. I replied that I had resolved to complete my education, as it was the wish of my mother when living, and was still the desire of my father, that I should. He then remarked that he had a gentleman friend who would want a good wife some time, and he would be pleased to introduce him on the morrow, if agreeable to me. I replied that I should certainly be pleased to form the acquaintance of his friend, and inquired his name. He replied it was Mr. Goodspeed. "Goodspeed, Goodspeed," said I to myself. "Where have I ever heard that name?" And, for the life of me, I could not recollect.

The morrow came: it was New-year's-day; a fine New England winter day. A new and deep snow had fallen.

As I looked out of my window in the morning upon the beautiful white crystals, as they lay snugly banked together, I could but think it was in harmony with the purity of soul of my dear friends who were about to be joined in the holy bands of matrimony.

Evening came, and the invited guests early assembled, and at the appointed time Mr. Shepherd and Rose came into the room. The guests all arose as they entered, and welcomed them. Soon after the performance of the wedding ceremony, the friends who were invited to the reception began to arrive, and the festivities of the occasion were continued until a late hour in the evening.

Mr. Shepherd was true to his promise, and introduced me to his friend Mr. Goodspeed. I found him a very agreeable gentleman, and very attentive; and, upon parting that evening, he requested the privilege of corresponding with me, which I freely granted, as there need not, of necessity, any evil result from it, for I could discontinue it at any time.

The day after the wedding I left for the seminary, and as I parted from Mr. and Mrs. Blackwell, and Rose and her husband, they poured forth a flood of tears; and, loading me with valuable presents as a more substantial testimony of their love, I was taken to the train in their sleigh, and was soon on my way back to school. I reached there in safety before nightfall. The next day I resumed my studies.

Nothing soon occurred of unusual interest, except it may be a correspondence between Mr. Goodspeed and myself.

A few days after my return from the wedding, I received the following:

"No. — School Street,
"Boston, January 6, 18—.

"MY DEAR MISS ASPASIA HORTON:—Referring to the few happy moments I was permitted to enjoy your company at the brilliant wedding of our mutual friends, at Mr. Blackwell's, in this city, a few days since, and your kindness in permitting me to open a correspondence with you, I now venture to address you; and, I confess, it is not without serious misgivings that I do so. Your friend Rose, now Mrs. Shepherd, has spoken of you in such exalted terms that I fear an uncultured expression may find a place upon this sheet and be detected by your quick vision and scholarly attainments. I need not assure you of my profound regard,—nay, more, of my most ardent love,—and I beg the privilege of frequent correspondence, trusting my expressions of esteem and love may find a response in your heart, and that you will favor me with your letters as oft as possible.

"Anxiously awaiting your reply,

"I am affectionately yours,

"MORGAN GOODSPEED."

On reading the letter, I burst into a loud laugh. "What a goose!" said I to myself. "My most ardent love!" *ha! ha!* "Well, well," thought I, "this is Young America, surely. Never saw him but once, nor he me; and yet he not only entertains 'profound regard' for me, but even loves me most ardently." Said I to myself, "Young gentleman, if your heart is so vulnerable, you may get fooled one of these days."

My way always is, if I have anything undone that is to be done, to at once set about doing it. So, when I receive letters from friends, I answer them immediately, and this for two or three reasons: first, the news conveyed in the letter received, and to which I am to reply, is always of more interest to me while fresh than after it has lain upon my table for a week, and therefore it is that I can indite an answer of more interest to my friend; and, second, if I reply immediately to a letter received, my friend takes it as evidence on my part that I appreciate his letter; and, third, upon the general principle, which has ever been the rule of my life, "whatsoever thy hand findeth to do, do it with all thy might."

Acting upon this principle, I said to myself, "Although I think Mr. Goodspeed a little imprudent, yet he may be honest, at all events. He is the friend of Mr. and Mrs. Shepherd, and I must reply: so here it goes." And I scribbled off the following:

"―――― SEMINARY, January 9, 18―.

" MORGAN GOODSPEED, ESQ., ― School Street, Boston:

" MY DEAR SIR:―Your favor of the 6th came by to-day's mail, and I have just read it with interest.

" With pleasure does my mind revert to the brilliant party at Mr. Blackwell's, and I am pleased to offer you expressions of gratitude and esteem for your courteous and gentlemanly attentions at that wedding, and especially as I was but a country lady amidst the sparkling city belles. But your letter flatters me. I really feel as though either your judgment is at fault, or I must have unconsciously put on counterfeit charms; for I cannot conceive why, amidst all the splendor that was shown forth by the ladies that evening, you should, in reality, have become so enamored of me. So far as future correspondence is concerned, I should not, for the present, object; for, if we can be of any real service to each other, we shall both be in the discharge of our duty.

" Be pleased to remember me to Mr. and Mrs. Shepherd as you have opportunity,

" And accept my high regards.

" Truly, yours,

" ASPASIA HORTON."

Being upon the last half of my last year at the seminary, I was just commencing the study of mental philosophy, moral science, geology, and history of literature, besides perfecting my Latin and Greek readings; consequently, I was compelled to work very hard at my studies, and, until near the close of the term, I declined all invitations to visit out of the seminary.

One afternoon I found a note from the principal, Miss Haywood, on my table, to the effect that she wished to meet the young ladies of the seminary to converse upon general topics of interest and to a general debate, intending it for the development of their argumentative powers, and, if they possessed any talents in that direction, she would endeavor to make it both pleasant and profitable; that but three or four ladies could argue upon a subject each evening, while the others could listen, and decide the question at the close. That the first meeting would be held in the large hall that evening, and she had designated myself, with two other young ladies and herself, to carry on the debate; that I must not fail to attend; she would announce the subject for discussion at the opening of the meeting.

I looked through my portfolio, found the letter received from my dear father that morning, and hastily answering it, handed it to the postman, who just then called for letters for the mail, and prepared myself for tea.

# CHAPTER VII.

Evening came, and I repaired to the large hall, and found the young ladies all assembled.

A table and four chairs stood in the center of the hall. Miss Haywood was seated at the table, leisurely turning the leaves of a book, apparently reading, but really to relieve herself from the gaze of the young ladies who were seated around the room.

Shortly after I entered, she arose from her seat, and addressed the meeting in a short speech, as follows:

"It has been a deep study with me how, or in what manner, or by what process, I can be instrumental in fitting my young ladies for society. What is needed in the education of young ladies is a moral and intellectual training to take the place of the dancing-school and fit them to adorn the parlor or drawing-room. If, with their knowledge of the arts and sciences, they could, by practice, acquire the faculty to communicate that knowledge with ease and grace, they would find themselves the center of attraction at every social entertainment; for in every company there are found those who are fond of discussion, some for diversion, some to hear themselves talk, 'and who e'en though vanquished will argue still,' and others from a desire to acquire and impart information; and though a large portion of the company may be gay, light-headed, and trifling, yet they will respect a sound reasoner nevertheless.

( 79 )

" It is for this purpose, young ladies, that I have called this meeting ; I propose to hold others once each week during the remainder of the term, as one of the regular exercises of the seminary.

"I shall not, in any case, give intimation of the subject to be discussed until at the opening of each meeting ; for my object is to stimulate your conversational powers and make you ready talkers."

She then named the debaters for that evening (myself being one of them), requesting them to be seated at the table. On taking our seats, she announced the following subject for discussion, viz.:

"Which are the most potent, the seen or the unseen forces ?"

"Miss Julia and myself will assume that the seen forces are the most potent, and Aspasia and Bell may argue in favor of the potency of the unseen forces.

" And, to proceed, in support of my theory that the seen forces are the most powerful, I am not to be confined to my own limited vision, but to range through history,—at least, to search it so far as the limited time will allow.

"In glancing over the history of the dead past, we start with the achievements of the ancient Egyptians. The erection of those vast monuments of grandeur and power, mounting up to heaven, even the modus operandi of their construction, is far beyond our comprehension : yet it was a seen force which transported those immense blocks across the sea and elevated them to so great altitudes. Again, visit with me that rich and elegant city, Babylon, the boastful queen of cities. The accounts we have from history of its wealth, its immense walls, its vast extent, its magnificence, are more like Oriental fancy than real historical facts. Walls that were originally over three hundred feet high, seventy-five feet broad, and sixty miles in circumference. One temple (Baal, or Belus) was half a mile in circuit, and forty rods, or six hundred and sixty-three feet, in height. And for the gratification of one of its queens, who had been brought from the mountains of Persia, her lord, the monarch of the city, erected hanging gardens in the midst of the plain, tier after tier resting upon arch above arch, all covered to a great depth with the rich soil of the plain, and planted with the floral beauties of all lands, this mighty and splendid artificial mountain towering far above the walls of the city, and, consequently, overlooking the vast plain of the Euphrates. Add to this the hundred massive gates of brass which protected the city on the river side. Then, again, its artificial lake, forty miles square, just outside the city.

"And was not all this grandeur and magnificence of art the result of seen forces?

"Then come down with me to the time of the Grecians, when art was in its perfection. Behold the beautiful temple of Diana, one of the wonders of the world, exceeding in magnificence anything within our conception. Also the Parthenon, celebrated the world over for the beauty of its architecture, grandeur, and magnificence of design. Cross over with me to Rome, and view St. Peter's, the wonder and admiration of the world.

"Were not all these the production of seen forces? Did not the labor and skill of man accomplish all this?

"Come down with me to more modern times. Formerly, the only means of communication between persons at a distance was by posts or signals, and history was written in hieroglyphics. But the genius of man— a seen force—established, and put in successful operation, the printing-press, by which history is recorded with the rapidity of thought. Yes, and by the operation of the telegraph two continents, separated by the mighty Atlantic, are brought together; and men, sitting in their offices thousands of miles apart, with the broad ocean intervening, may talk with each other freely and rapidly.

"Behold the wonderful bridges spanning mighty rivers and fearful gulfs, dangling in the air like the string of a boy's kite; yet they sustain and bear across safely immense railway-trains. Do the people of one of our cities desire pure water, they hesitate not to tunnel for miles under an inland sea, and thus draw from an inexhaustible fountain.

"And is not all this the work and accomplishment of man, a seen force?

"Examine the manufactured fabrics, woolen, cotton, silk, and worsted, in all variety of colors, shades, and designs. Go into those factories. Examine the machinery, which, apparently, operates by its own volition.

"And is not all this the accomplishment of the seen force?

"I trust, ladies, that I have succeeded in establishing in your minds the fact of the greater potency of the seen over the unseen forces."

Miss Haywood took her seat amidst the waving of handkerchiefs and clapping of hands.

She then called upon Bell to answer her.

Bell excused herself by saying "the arguments presented seemed to have exhausted the subject, and she dared not venture a reply."

Miss Haywood then called upon me.

I replied that "the closing argument belonged to me, her colleague, Miss Julia, might proceed with her argument, and I would close the debate."

Miss Julia, rising, said, "I shall not trespass upon your time and patience but for one moment. I cannot say anything to strengthen the case so ably presented by my colleague in this argument, and can only add that I deem them conclusive; and, in view of the rapid progress made through the agency of the seen forces in the past, we may believe that such development will be greatly accelerated in the future."

It now devolved upon me to close the discussion. It was not without great misgivings that I arose, and, wiping the perspiration from my brow, I spoke as follows:

"Young ladies, in discussing this important proposition, which has been so ably argued on the other side by our lady principal, I must ask your patience and forbearance; for, as you are aware, I was wholly ignorant of the subject to be discussed, while, at the same time, it is at least presumable, from the masterly manner in which she has opened the debate, that she had thoroughly considered the subject. Be that as it may, I shall endeavor to prove, by argument and sound philosophy, that the position assumed by my opponent is untenable, that the unseen forces are vastly more potent and effective than the seen; and, in discussing this, I am free to acknowledge my obligations to my opponents for opening up so wide a range for argument; for while they have traversed considerably outside the theme actually under discussion, it warrants me, in my reply, to follow them into the unexplored fields suggested by their arguments, and thus be enabled to show more clearly not only the effects or results of the unseen forces, but what may be anticipated in the future.

"We read, 'In the beginning God created the heaven and the earth; and the earth was without form, and void.' And God said, Let there be light; and there was light.'

"Now, then, has any argument been presented to us this evening to prove that any seen force is, or ever was, able to call a world into being from chaos, and clothe that world with living splendor and people it with immortal souls?

"And was it not an unseen force which accomplished all this? Has any one ever seen God? And is he not the great unseen force which sustains, rules, and guides the world?

"My opponent has referred, in brilliant language, to the temple of Belus reaching up to heaven; to the splendor and magnificence of Babylon and its wonderful hanging gardens, over three hundred feet in height; to the temples of Minerva and Diana, that were the wonder and admiration of the world; to the Church of St. Peter's at Rome; and to the glorious achievements of men in more modern times. And her arguments were poured forth in such strains of eloquence that, were it not for the consciousness that the eternal principles of truth are on my side, I should have shrunk from even attempting a reply.

"But she could have added to her list of works of art of astounding magnificence, the productions of man (the seen force) *ad infinitum;* for the Old World is full of ruins which bespeak the potency not of the seen force, but of the unseen.

"Many of those surprising works of art referred to have perished. Admit, for argument's sake only, that they were the creations of the seen force. How comes it that they have perished? Because of the far greater potency of an unseen force. Neglected and forsaken by men, that mysterious unseen force has been quietly and silently crumbling them all to dust. Many of the most stupendous works referred to are so completely destroyed that no vestige of them remains.

"My opponent might with equal propriety have offered as proof the magnificence of the cities of Herculaneum and Pompeii, with all their statues and elegant paintings. But were these not all destroyed in an hour by an unseen force, when Vesuvius first uttered a groan as if writhing with pain, and, opening its mouth, belched forth a flood of fire and lava, burying those ill-fated cities? Was it not an unseen force? And has any one ever looked down into the bowels of that grand old mountain, and seen the force which vomited out that liquid fire? Surely not. And, since the creation of the world, has there been so powerful an exhibition of the seen forces as that awful catastrophe? No, never!

"I admit that art, in its grandeur, was apparently perfected in the times and cities of the Old World; but was not that also the product of an unseen force in the soul of man, moving him on to the accomplishment of those grand and elegant works of art?

"We are told by the debaters on the other side that the elegance of our manufactured fabrics is another exhibition of the potency of the seen forces. Why? Because, forsooth, those machines which seem to perform those wonderful feats as if by their own volition, were the device and workmanship of man; and those machines, in performing their manipulations, are, we are told, seen forces. This I most distinctly deny; on the contrary, they are no forces at all. Were they forces, they would never cease their operations. But we find that so soon as the actual force which propels them is withdrawn or withheld, they are silent and inactive; and even those machines were not, as is claimed, the result of seen force, but of the unseen. The mind of man, that mysterious unseen force, devised, wrought out, and put them in operation.

"As I look out of my window, a snow-storm is wrapping the cold earth in its soft and fleecy fold. One by one, flake after flake, in quick succession, drops out of the dark and mysterious ethereal space and takes its place upon the ground.

"The darkness of night comes on. Silently and softly the little crystals continue to drop during the night.

"I arise in the morning, and immense snow-banks have formed, which require the labor of men and teams for days to remove sufficient for a passage. Now, will my opponent tell us if any one has ever seen that force which was the cause of all this?

"Spring-time has come, and the meadows are growing green. From day to day I watch the growth of the grass. Silently and most mysteriously it continues, until it is ready for the harvest, and is then garnered into barns to nourish and sustain animal life during another cold and dreary winter. Has any one seen the power which causes all this? No! It is a secret unseen force far beyond our comprehension.

"The night is cold and cheerless; morning dawns; the atmosphere is cool and bracing. The day is lovely. The sun in the heavens shines forth with its wonted brilliancy and splendor. Mid-day comes, and the intense heat causes the flocks and herds to seek the shade; the farmer unhitches his team and leads them to the stalls, and himself retires 'neath the shade to rest until the heat of the day is over. Hark! I hear a distant sound, as of thunder. A small cloud is seen crawling up the western horizon. It increases rapidly in size, until yonder heavens are as black as night; and from out that dark and mysterious cloud I see fire darting forth, and with peal after peal the artillery of heaven pours forth its volleys. The clouds overshadow the earth; and where, but a half-hour since, all was beautiful, now all is awfully sublime and fearfully grand. The storm rages; the lightnings flash and dart athwart the heavens; the grand old oaken forests, that have withstood the storms of centuries, bow their heads, and are swept to the ground by this storm-king. Cities and villages which lie in its path, that required the labor of thousands of men (seen forces) to erect and embellish, are, in a single hour, totally demolished by this terrible unseen force.

"I trust, ladies, that I have convinced you that the unseen forces are vastly more potent than the seen."

The debate being closed, Miss Haywood arose, and, addressing herself to the audience, said,

"Young ladies, the arguments of Aspasia are conclusive. I admit myself vanquished. I am convinced, as I know you must all be, by the powerful arguments presented by my opponent as to the power of the unseen over the seen forces."

At this announcement the young ladies arose with a shout and clapping of hands. Flowers and bouquets were thrown at my feet. Thus ended the first lyceum meeting in the seminary.

To detail my experience during the remainder of the term would be uninteresting; and I will only briefly refer to some further correspondence with Mr. Goodspeed.

As seen by the date of the letter, it was not until the middle of February that I again heard from him; and I supposed that in criticising my letter he had concluded that his most " ardent love" expressions did not meet with a full and hearty response, and that he would venture no further; but at last I received the following:

"My dear Aspasia:—Your dignified yet courteous letter of the 9th ultimo reached me by due course of mail, and my long silence has, without doubt, awakened serious apprehensions in your mind; but when you come to learn the real cause of my delay in answering your very precious letter, you will overlook the seeming negligence.

"I received yours late in the afternoon, and had but just read it when I received a telegram from New Orleans that a merchant whom our house had trusted for large amounts was about to make an assignment, and prefer his creditors at the South, and if one of the members of our house would come on there at once we could save the debt. Looking at my watch, I saw I had but ten minutes in which to reach the train. I said to my partner, 'Mr. Hammond, have the book-keeper forward to me at New Orleans, by to-morrow morning's express, Mr. ——'s account; also take my keys (handing them to him), go to my hotel and pack my satchel, and forward that at the same time. I will keep you advised of my success.' In a few moments I reached the depot, just in season to jump on board the cars as they were passing out, and was then on my way to New Orleans, whither I reached in safety; my satchel did not reach me for three days after. And, since I have felt it necessary to detail this trip, it may not be uninteresting to you to know that I succeeded in securing the entire debt. Finding that I had outgeneraled him, and that there was no possible way of escape, he got his friends to see me and obtain a proposition for discounting the debt. This he was compelled to do, or utterly fail, without an opportunity to pocket a single dollar, as with my legal process I had been able to seize upon his entire stock in

trade, and it was sure. I proposed to discount ten per
cent. for cash, which was readily accepted, and the money
paid me,—forty-two thousand and four hundred dollars. After settling with my attorney, and reserving
sufficient for my expenses, I remitted the remainder to
my house.

"I was so completely absorbed in this undertaking that
I could not find a moment's time to write.

"This is my excuse for not writing sooner, which I
doubt not will appear reasonable and sufficient to you.

"I arrived home this morning, very much fatigued, yet
not so but that I can spend an hour in writing you.

"Permit me to philosophize for a moment upon a creature we call man,—a business-man, if you please.

"When I first commenced in business, I thought that
if a customer from the South or West, while purchasing
a bill of goods, should inquire what church I attended,
and if I could inform him at what hour the Sabbath-
school was held, and whether such and such a church
had Wednesday evening meetings, it would be perfectly
safe to trust such a person for all he would purchase; but,
alas! as Widow Bedott says, 'man is a poor weak critter;'
or, as another who has written of him most elegantly
styles him, 'a poor fellow.' This customer of mine was
one of that class, a 'wolf arrayed in sheep's clothing,'
'stealing the livery of heaven to serve the devil in.' He
pretended to be an elder in a Presbyterian church; and
yet scarcely a business-man in New Orleans who is not
a relative of his would believe him under oath. Does
it not indeed seem very strange that men can become so
wicked? I have never professed religion, and for years
did not attend church, and I feasted on what I termed
the sins of Christians; but when I came to investigate

8*

this case I found that Christianity was in no way responsible for it. To scan my own acts and judgments, I have come to the conclusion that, in a measure at least, I have been in the wrong. In my experience I have also learned that men—yes, and women also—are not always the same abroad as they are at home. Here, too, 'is an evil under the sun.' But the facilities for quick communication between distant parts of the country are now so great, and there are so many more people traveling than formerly, that a man has to be more careful how he deports himself while away from home than a few years since, lest he may be seen by his neighbors and they communicate to his friends. I look upon this as one of the great safeguards of our young country merchants in coming to the city to make purchases; and is among the means employed by Providence to correct evil habits and stimulate to nobler thoughts and deeds.

"Leaving this subject, as quite likely it may be uninteresting to your finely cultivated mind, I wish to reiterate my expressions of ardent attachment to you. I do not think, as you intimate, 'that my judgment was at fault,' nor that you 'put on counterfeit charms.' I have lived quite long in fashionable life, for one of my years. My experience in society has been extensive; and I have never, in a single instance, been deceived in my estimate of a lady's character and talents. This is no egotism, and I feel justified, under the circumstances, in making the statement. True, there were ladies at the wedding who were dressed more elegantly than yourself, and, so far as trinkets were an adornment, far outshone you. Yet in the matter of true, genuine adornment of grace and refinement, with a cultured intellect and a mind trained by education to take life like a true philosopher, and apparently without an envious thought, you seemed the perfection of woman to me; and I am not yet willing to admit that my conclusions were incorrect. I am anxious to test it by yet more intimate acquaintanceship.

" I met Mr. Shepherd just as I reached my store, and gave him and for his loving wife your regards. Although long since made, I took it for granted you had not rescinded the order. He wished me to return his and Mrs. Shepherd's regards to you.

" I beg of you to reply at once. Give me a good long letter, and write everything that has transpired since I saw you that you think will be of interest to me.

" And believe me, truly and affectionately yours,  ·
"MORGAN GOODSPEED."

After reading this letter carefully, and closely criticising the line of thought developed, I said to myself, " Neither am I mistaken. Mr. Goodspeed is evidently a gentleman of sagacity, sound judgment, close, discriminating mind, warm-hearted, generous, and impulsive, and is deserving of a good wife." But, as for me, I could not and would not think of such a thing, for sister Elizabeth was just about to be married, and I should have to go home and take care of father, being fully resolved never to leave him alone. I therefore wrote Mr. Goodspeed, expressing profound respect and admiration for him, thanking him most generously for his favors, and saying that, from the fact that I should be intensely occupied with my studies during the remainder of the term, and for other reasons as herein stated, I felt it a duty to himself to discontinue the correspondence with this letter.

The result was, that in about a week I received a letter from Rose (Mrs. Shepherd), in which she gave me a good scolding, and promised to visit me after my return

At last term closed, and with it I graduated with high honors,—the first in my class.

And, bidding good-by to my alma mater and the loved ones with whom I had for three long years associated with no unkind word or thought, I departed for my home.

# CHAPTER VIII.

HAVING completed my education, I had returned home fully determined to remain with my dear father so long as he desired,—at least, never to leave him permanently, should an opportunity offer, without first seeing that he was well provided for.

This resolve was rendered necessary, at least in part, by the fact that sister Elizabeth was about to be married; indeed she was married within a few weeks after my return from the seminary; and I am pleased to know that she married well; in fact, her husband possessed a high order of talents, and in all respects was a splendid gentleman. And it pained me to observe, as I did in after-years, that my sister did not appreciate him; being of an opposite temperament, with habits of thought and ideas of propriety widely differing from her husband, she was a constant hindrance to him. I shall endeavor to give an impartial review hereafter of some portions of their married life as it came under my observation; for there are valuable lessons to be learned from their experiences.

Soon after my return, Laura Greenwood was married, and went West to reside. She and Bell Jones spent only one year in the seminary.

I found, on returning home, that I had more friends in town than I had supposed; for during the past three years I had been at home but a small portion of the time, and during that time had grown in stature as well as ma-

ture in mind; and I found, on returning (and somewhat
to my surprise), that very many of the ladies,—yes, and of
the gentlemen also,—who looked upon me only as a little
girl and addressed me as Aspasia when I left home for the
seminary, now welcomed me back as Miss Horton; the
effect of which naturally caused me to put on something
of a dignified appearance.

But there was one exception to the ladies in the particular mentioned. That was Jane Fisher.

I first met Jane in church at the close of the morning
service on the first Sabbath after my return. She came
rushing up to me, "Aspasia Horton! Well, if you
ain't grown, I'll give it up! Come home to stay? Did
you graduate? Get a diploma? What luck did you have
with your studies? How high did you rank in your
class? Have you any idea of getting married? I heard
you had. Now, if it is so, tell me, and then I shall know;
and if you ain't, say so, for I know you'll tell the truth;.
and then I can tell folks."

"Yes," thought I,—"'tell folks.' News is what she
is after." She was so impatient to learn everything that
she conceived possible for any person to inquire about,
that she hardly had time to take breath between her interrogatories, and I simply replied to each, as fast as put,
with yes or no, as the case might be. While she was pro-
pounding her questions, several ladies came to meet me
cordially, as they said I resembled my mother so much,
the memory of whose love and affection still lingered
with them; and they said they thought they saw her
image reflected in me. They all addressed me as Miss
Horton. "No," said Jane: "it's Aspasia, and nothing
else, with me."

By this time sister Kate and her husband came and
relieved me, for I then had an excuse to get away from

Jane and avoid any further quizzing and questioning. As I left, I overheard one of the women say, "How much she looks and acts like her mother! I hope she won't get married right off, as all the rest of Mr. Horton's children have, except William."

"No," said Jane; "she hain't no notion of being married; she told me so. And I'm glad I asked her; for now I can tell folks."

"Well," thought I, "this matter will be pretty well settled before night, unless something serious should happen to Jane."

I had been so little accustomed to house-work that it came pretty hard upon me at first to have the care of the family. True, we had a good kitchen-girl; and I have often thought that she (who really understood the work at first very much better than myself) was more patient in teaching me than most girls would have been, and I have ever remembered her with gratitude.

As I became more familiar with household cares, so I came to relish and enjoy such employments; and I found that physical exercise was the very thing I needed, for, by my habits of intense thought and close study, I had become somewhat dyspeptic, and, consequently, was not so buoyant in spirit as previously. But I soon found that, as the result of active exercise and getting very tired some days, my digestion was wholly restored, my wonted buoyancy returned, my drooping spirits revived, and I could think clearly and rapidly; and in all respects I began to feel like a new creature.

My father's crops were abundant that season. Consequently, he employed several hired men; and in harvest especially I was kept very busy. My lady readers in the country will appreciate my situation at this time.

Autumn at last came. As William returned from

town one evening, he handed me a letter. I opened it, and, glancing at the signature, saw it was from my friend Rose (Mrs. Shepherd). I laid it aside to prepare tea for William (for he had been out all day, and it was now quite late). After he had taken his tea, I read my letter, which was as follows:

"Boston, November 18, 18—.

"MY DEAR ASPASIA:—It has been a long, long time since I have heard from you; and I have waited until, by and with the advice and urgent solicitations of my dear husband, I have concluded to write you; and, as the Irishman wrote to a long-absent friend, 'If you're dead, git your brother to answer this letter.' So I say. If you cannot write, do get some one to reply for you. But, joking aside, I wish to know when it will be the most convenient for you to have me visit you. I have made up my mind to do so early, for I have some very important things to say to you, which I cannot write.

"I should have visited you ere this had I not been prevented by circumstances entirely beyond my control; and these same circumstances also prevented my writing; and, besides all this, we (husband and myself) have received a very precious present this fall, which I wish you to see, for I know you will appreciate it. I cannot describe it to you, and shall bring it with me when I visit you.

"Mr. Goodspeed was in this evening, and spent an hour very agreeably, although he is quite low-spirited. Your last letter to him was a crusher, and I do think you were cruel. But enough of that now. I remarked to him that I was about to write you; and he wished me to remember him affectionately to you. By-the-way, he says he knows more of you than he thought. He has met a lady friend of his who says you are the lady they (herself and Mr. Goodspeed) spent an evening with at the sea-side three summers ago, when you preached them a sermon. And he said, further, that he had never forgotten it, and never should; that previous to that evening he had been a skeptic, but abandoned his skepticism entirely after listening to your arguments.

"My husband joins me in expressions of sincere affection.

"Please reply to this at once,

"And believe me, as ever,

"Yours,

"ROSE."

I had been so thoroughly occupied in my new calling that I had almost forgotten my friends. No, I had not forgotten them, but I had neglected them; and the receipt of this letter brought vividly to my mind the reminiscences of other days; the happy hours spent with friends, many of whom had gone,—either died or moved away.

After conferring with father and William, it was thought best to write her to come at once,—which I did, requesting her to telegraph the morning she left, and William would meet her at the depot with a carriage.

In about one week we received a dispatch that she would arrive on the afternoon train; and William met her at the depot.

I was standing at the south window as I saw them emerge from the pine-woods; and, on driving up to the door, I observed Rose had a bundle in her arms. I ran to the gate to welcome her, and she handed me her bundle, saying, "Handle it carefully; it is the present I wrote

9

you about." I took it, and, lo and behold, it was a bouncing baby boy !

"Bless your soul, Rose," said I, "is this yours ?"

"Most certainly it is," she replied; "and he is worth ten times his weight in gold; and you will say so when you come to see him."

On going into the house I undid the baby, and, sure enough, he was a noble boy. Said I, "Rose Shepherd, this is just like you. Just such a baby as I should suppose you would have. A noble head, fair and express-ive countenance, fine, clear blue eyes, and a heart nat-urally full of generous impulses. A splendid baby ! But," said I, "come to your room. John, bring up that trunk."

Soon Rose came down to the parlor. My father coming in just then, I introduced him. He remarked that he was very glad to welcome her, as she was a friend of mine; and his love was so fervent for me that he felt himself instinctively impelled by emotions of love toward my friends.

Rose thanked him, and replied that, aside from her dear husband, she had no friend for whom she cherished such undying love as for Aspasia.

In the afternoon of the second day of Rose's visit, while sitting at the parlor-fire, talking of the scenes of other days, of our experiences at the seminary, the circumstances of her wedding, etc.; said she, "Aspasia, I wrote you that I had something important to say to you; and as we are now alone, the baby is asleep, and the storm without will prevent visitors, suppose we talk it over now."

"Well," said I, "proceed,"—which she did, as follows:

"Last March, Mr. Goodspeed showed me the letter he had received from you, saying that, for certain reasons, you thought best to discontinue the correspondence. I read the letter, and confess I thought it pretty cool, and wrote you accordingly, but by his earnest wish.

"He asked me if I did not think it coquettish to jilt a gentleman after that style.

"'No,' said I; 'I know Aspasia too well for that. There is none of the coquette about her; and that is the worst feature there is about it: she is in real earnest.'

"'Well,' he replied, 'it seems as though I could not have it so. But I suppose I must submit, unless you can intercede in my behalf.'

"I then promised him that I would make you a visit and talk the matter over with you.

"You recollect I wrote that circumstances entirely beyond my control had prevented my visiting you earlier. The explanation of that is lying snugly, and as sweet as an angel, in that cradle" (pointing to it).

"Now, then, I wish you to reconsider your resolution, and give me authority to invite Mr. Goodspeed to visit you while I am here, and then you and he can agree upon your future course. And I am free to give you my reasons for urging this proposition.

"First, you are twenty years of age, and you certainly ought not to defer marriage longer than sufficient time to make due preparations for the wedding after a good offer is made you.

"And, second, Mr. Goodspeed is ready at any time to offer you his hand and heart.

"And, again, I believe he will make you a devoted husband. He is kind, affable, large-hearted, and full of sympathy, and is, as you are aware, very fine-looking. My husband says he is also a first-class business-man, and is, pecuniarily, quite well off; so that you will never want for the comforts, and even luxuries, of life.

"Now, then, what more could you wish? I know what

you will say. He is not a Christian. No; but I believe that, by the grace of God, you could make him
one. He has spoken many times of that sermon (as he
calls it) that you gave him and his lady friend at the
sea-side, and of the impressions it left upon his mind; and
he says his life has been quite different since, and, as I
wrote you, he is actually growing melancholy and sad.
He has called at our house as often as every other day, to
learn when I should visit you, and, when I left home, he
remarked that he should be quite impatient to hear from
me, as I promised to write him after conferring with you."

"Well," said I, "Rose, you will beat the lawyers in
special pleading. With such an advocate, Mr. Goodspeed
most certainly ought to succeed; and I don't know but he
may. But I cannot decide to-day; and I tell you what I
wish you to do. I will call father in this evening after
tea, and you speak your piece to him, and see what he
says. I will then talk with him about it, and let you know
the result."

Evening came, and, after tea, we all repaired to the
parlor, except brother William, who had to attend a meeting of the town officers that evening, as he was a member
of the board.

Being seated around the fire, I reminded father of my
correspondence, while in the seminary (which he was
then aware of), with a Mr. Goodspeed, a gentleman I
met at Mrs. Shepherd's wedding, and that some time previous to my leaving the seminary I caused a suspension
of hostilities, for the reason that my mind was thoroughly
occupied with my studies, and, moreover, I was about to
come home and stay with him (my father).

"Now, Mr. Goodspeed is a friend of Mr. and Mrs.
Shepherd, and Mrs. Shepherd has been making a forcible
plea to me to invite Mr. Goodspeed here at once while she

is with us, and I told her that she might speak her piece to you this evening, and see what you would say to it. So, Rose, you may proceed."

She then repeated the same to father she had said to me, word for word, as though she had learned it by heart.

After listening to her earnestly, father leaned forward, resting his elbows on his knees, with his head in his hands, and appeared to be in deep thought for several moments; and finally, wiping the tears from his eyes, and turning toward me, said he, "Aspasia, I don't know how I can live without you; but possibly I may not live long anyway, and I think, on the whole, you had better let Mrs. Shepherd send for him to come here. I can tell in a very short time whether it will be worth his while to come more than once."

Accordingly, I consented, and Rose called for writing-materials, which father brought, and she hastily wrote a brief note, and had it ready for the post in the morning.

About this time brother William returned from town; and, after discussing the news brought home by him,—it getting late,—we all retired for the night.

9*

# CHAPTER IX.

"Whence holiness of will derives its birth,
Whence piety and faith illumine earth,
'Gainst men ungrateful, of false virtue vain,
I sing; a thousand verses form the strain.
If, reader, to such knowledge you aspire,
Search here, and gratify your good desire.
From frantic errors safe, the growth of pride;
These, if you study well, will be your guide;
Nor will you dare against the God of grace
Rebellious human liberty to place.
Nor will you any of his gifts disown;
Nor think you merit, but by Him alone;
Whate'er is good in you, you here will trace,
Not as the cause, but the effect, of grace."

In a few days we had the pleasure of welcoming Mr. Goodspeed at our house.

Mrs. Shepherd took him aside privily, soon after his arrival (as she afterward informed me), and told him to be sure and get on the right side of my father, and he would be all right; for if my father advised me to marry him I would do so.

Thus being placed upon his guard at the very outset of the conflict, he would have been a dull soldier had he failed in taking the castle.

A day or two after his arrival, father and William both spent the day in the house, on account of a severe December storm.

William was occupied the greater part of the day in posting his account-books; for he attended to his bookkeeping entirely of evenings and stormy days. The rest of us were in the parlor. The storm was raging furiously without, and we were all cosily seated around a comfortable fire.

The circumstances were such as to call forth the exercise of our social powers and cause us all to throw off reserve ; and the result was a lively and interesting conversation during nearly the entire day.

I have observed, in my experience, that at certain times and under peculiar circumstances it is very much easier to approach strangers and draw them out in conversation, than at other times.

A stormy day is one.

Waiting at a depot in the night for a train that is past due is another.

I well remember going to the depot one stormy evening to meet some friends expected on the train. A gentleman passed me repeatedly, in a nervous, restless manner. At last, approaching me, he remarked, " Train is behind time; I fear some accident may have happened. Are you expecting friends?" I replied, " Yes," and inquired if he was. He said, " Yes,—my wife and child; and I fear something has happened to the train." He then entered into conversation as freely as though we were familiar acquaintances. At last I ventured to inquire his name, and was greatly surprised to learn that it was the Hon. ——, who was celebrated more than any thing else for his reserve and dignity, and was rarely ever seen stooping so low as to converse with any one less than a governor or a judge.

But the truth was, he was one of that class whose whole life was counterfeit. Such do not live their own natures at all. He was naturally courteous and genial ; and the circumstances under which I met him were those

calculated to develop his real character. He was anticipating trouble, fearing an accident had happened to the
train, and that his dear wife and child were injured; and,
finding I was also expecting friends by the same train,
he quite likely said to himself, "Now I can find sympathy:" he therefore at once and without reserve threw
off his mask, and played the original part assigned by
Nature.

On board a vessel during a storm is another occasion
for developing the genial qualities of humanity.

I have experienced such; and it is really amusing to
see how affable persons become under such circumstances, who but an hour previous were haughty and
self-opinionated,—even disgustingly so.

But to return to our subject. The conversation commenced by Mr. Goodspeed relating a few incidents which
happened on the train he came on, and which were referred to by him to sustain his theory that a railroad-car
was the best place in the world in which to study human
nature. He said that during the day two women came
into the car, every seat was fully occupied, and they
were compelled to stand, until he suggested to the gentleman who sat beside him that they give the ladies their
seats, which was agreed to, whereupon they took possession at once, but without the least acknowledgments
for the favor. The two gentlemen were compelled to
stand for a whole hour. At last, arriving at their stations, the women left the seats and hastened to the door.
Just as they were stepping upon the platform, he cried
out to them, "Ladies, you have forgotten something."
They both ran back to the seat hurriedly, and inquired
what they had left. He replied, "You forgot to thank
us for your seats, as ladies should." They sneaked out
of the car amid a roar of laughter from all the passengers.

My father remarked that he had traveled by railway considerable, and had himself thought it a good place to study human nature, until he was led to criticise his own acts, when he found that the selfish principle in his nature was much more largely developed while traveling than while at home. He was therefore compelled to entertain charitable feelings toward others.

I remarked that, so far as my experience went, I thought there was more truth than poetry in the aphorism, "This world is all a cattle-show." "And so it is," I went on. "As the farmer takes only his best cattle to the fair, so with people on exhibition or away from home: while under restraint they only exhibit the best traits in their character.

"It is also said that All the world's a stage.

"The question is, What kind of a stage? Is it a coach, using the compound term stage-coach, with a Jehu for a driver? If so, it is surely correct; for I believe there never was an era in the history of man when all the propelling forces, mental and physical, were so thoroughly taxed as now.

"It may be that a theater, or the stage in a theater, is meant by the expression. If so, it is correct; for in everyday life we see all the actors in appropriate costume, each in turn performing his part.

"We see the truly sincere and devout man, who has the least possible amount of selfishness, living for the good of others, controlled in his whole life by the golden rule of God.

"We see the sanctimonious hypocrite occupying one of the most expensive pews in the church, always laying his head forward reverently during prayers, and on the following Monday early fastening his claws, by a legal process, upon some poor unfortunate who is (in consequence of adversity) in arrears for one month's rent.

" We see the genial-faced gentleman, who is reputed as one of the most liberal men in the town; but his part is simply to be so while upon the stage, and he never plays unless before a good audience. He is sure never to give, except in a manner to have it known. If he is in church, and 'the box is passed around,' unlike other men, he has no money with him, which without ostentation he could give. No: he must call for a paper and pencil and write down his donation, with an order to call at his office and collect. He makes money by his reputation.

" The scene changes. Here comes the Jew, with his blue cotton umbrella under his arm, eager to light upon a Gentile customer, and, with a hellish grin, exhibits the liveliest emotion if his customer happens to be some unfortunate one whose home is mortgaged and time of redemption just about expired, and is willing to sacrifice the earnings of years of hard, honest toil to save a little, even, for his wife and children.

" Here comes the foppish gentleman, whose mustache is twisted into two elegant little pig-tails, pointing each way, as much as to say, ' If you are looking for brains, go somewhere else.' He struts, bows, and scrapes like a turkey-gobbler in spring-time. This chap never receives an encore.

" In striking contrast to the last actor, here comes the graceful, unaffected, urbane gentleman, whose very presence sends a thrill of joy through you,—that you have found a man.

" Then comes the plain, matter-of-fact man, using no satire, but dealing with the naked truth. Sanguine he may be, and, if so, frequently wounding the heart of many a friend, but also causing himself, at times, deep grief; yet, if lymphatic, he accomplishes really less good to society.

"Then here comes the buffoon. We find him in the pulpit, on the forum, at the bar, behind the counter, among our law-makers; wherever we go we find some one who feels it incumbent upon himself to play the part of the 'king's fool.'

"And last, but by no means the least, we have the sponge; the most despicable part in the play. In studying the plot carefully, one would suppose that few could be found to play so mean a part; but it is quite the reverse, and performers in it are never wanting. Always absorbing and never giving; and as the marine substance of that name varies in form, size, and color, and some are more porous than others, so with the men—yes, and the women also—who play the sponge on the stage of life. They exhibit all those varieties; and it is also their misfortune that, however well they play their parts, they are universally despised by all the other actors on the stage.

"And thus I might go on *ad infinitum*, and call up the actors in this drama of life, had I time."

"Well," said Mr. Goodspeed, "will you please assign me my part?"

"Not at all," I replied. "You have made, or, if not already, you will make, your own selection."

"But," said he, "in your opinion, which part am I the best adapted for?"

I begged he would excuse me, for I abhorred flattery, and did not wish to misjudge him, and, with his permission, I would withhold my answer until some future time; to which he consented. He then entered into conversation with my father upon politics, business, etc., in which I took comparatively little interest.

I observed one thing, however, that he seemed to agree with my father upon all points of any importance; he was particular not to commit himself on any proposition until he was well satisfied how my father stood upon that point.

And he played his part well, as the sequel will prove.

After our visitors had retired for the night, and my father and myself were sitting by the fire, waiting for the soapstone to heat (for I did not retire any night without first seeing him comfortably "tucked up" in bed), we sat in silence several moments. At last father broke the spell, and said he, "Aspasia, I guess you had better make up your mind to marry Mr. Goodspeed; he appears like a very fine gentleman, well informed, says he is quite wealthy, is good-looking, and seems to be a very moral man. I wish he was a Christian; but I think he is that sort of a man that if you marry him and are faithful he will become one; and, if he should, he will do a great deal of good. And surely you will not have to work at all, according to what he and Mrs. Shepherd say. And there is Elizabeth,—true, she has a first-rate husband, none better in the world; but then she complains, you know, because she has to work so hard about the house; her husband can't afford to keep two girls; and if you can marry a man with a fortune you had better do so."

"Father," said I, " I should be the most miserable creature on earth if I had nothing to do. Were I to marry a man as rich as Crœsus, I should work. For, in the first place, it is a part of my religion; it was a command that God gave to man, and made it imperative; and laziness I believe a sin. And as for sister Elizabeth,—true, she is not lazy, but she is very petulant and fault-finding: her husband's row is the hardest to hoe. If you think best, I will say to Mr. Goodspeed to-morrow, before he leaves for Boston, that he may resume the correspondence, and when I get time I can marry him or not, as I please. I sha'n't marry any one this winter: that's certain."

With this, father trudged off to bed, and, after seeing him snugly ensconced, I retired for the night.

Morning dawned. We arose early, as Mr. Goodspeed wished to return by the first train, and Mrs. Shepherd had concluded to return with him. We had breakfast early; and, while waiting for William to come with the sleigh, I said to Mr. Goodspeed that I should be pleased to resume our correspondence, and hoped to hear from him often, and should take great pleasure in reading and answering his letters.

And I must say that, judging from his looks and appearance, I never was conscious of contributing so much happiness to a person in so short a time, and in so few words, as then. He laughed all over, and, quick as thought, " by your permission," planted a kiss on my cheek; and, thanking me kindly, he remarked " that, although yesterday was a stormy, dreary day, yet it was the happiest day of his life, except this day."

In a few moments brother William came, and I saw them snugly stowed away in the sleigh; and, with a hearty good-by, they went whirling down the road. I watched them into the pine woods, and went about my morning's work.

Winter passed away, with nothing of very great importance occurring in which I was particularly interested, except that sister Kate brought her husband a beautiful bouncing boy. Mr. Shaw took it, as he did all his blessings, as providential.

It would be uninteresting to detail the correspondence that passed between Mr. Goodspeed and myself that winter and the spring and summer following.

The next season was very dry and warm, so that my

father's crops were cut off by the drought, as were the crops of all the neighboring farmers.

In the autumn a meeting was called at the town-house in the village, to see what plan could be devised to procure grain for the farmers to use during the winter; and the result of the meeting was, the contribution of from two to five hundred dollars each, by some fifty farmers, into a common fund, and the appointment of brother William as their agent to take this money and proceed West, and purchase and ship home flour and corn, which should be apportioned to each contributor according to the amount so paid in by him.

Accordingly, I made ready William's clothes; and, as soon as he could arrange his business, he left for Chicago.

It reminded me of good old Israel sending down into Egypt after corn, under the same circumstances: the dry weather had cut off his crops also. About the only difference between the two cases was, that in the first the farmers all went, while in this they sent an agent. But, as William left the house with father, I could but remember those mournful words of Jacob, " I shall see his face no more."

All of the fifty farmers who sent him were at the cars to see him safely off.

Mr. Shaw was also there; and, as the cars started, father said he heard him say, " May the Lord bless him and return him safe!" Then, turning to father, he remarked, " It's dangerous traveling, now, by rail, so many accidents are happening; but I hope he may have a safe trip." Father said it was spoken in such a manner, and came so unexpectedly, that it disturbed him a good deal.

We anxiously awaited letters, and were rejoiced to

learn of William's safe arrival at Chicago. And that he in due time completed his purchases satisfactorily, and informed us, by letter, that he should leave for home on a certain day and by a certain route.

He left as he had stated; and all went well until the second day. While the cars were running at a fearful speed (endeavoring to make up lost time), just as they came on to a high bridge, the train was thrown from the track by a broken rail, and precipitated into the chasm below ; and the cars, taking fire, were all burned, several passengers were killed outright by the fall, and others dreadfully mangled, and many burnt to death.

We learned of the accident the next day after its occurrence; and father and I rode to the village to see what people thought about brother William's being on that train. Several letters were produced by different persons, stating that he should leave Chicago by that route and upon such a day ; and the presumption was that he was on board of the ill-fated train. For he was known to be a man who always did just what he said he would. If he made an appointment to meet a person at a certain place or hour, he always fulfilled the appointment.

My father, in his deep anxiety that night, could not sleep, and neither could I ; but I dared not let him know that I was in the least apprehensive that evil had happened to William.

My room adjoined that of my father; and I could hear him cry out, in the night, "O God, spare me the deep affliction which I fear." And, after turning himself repeatedly in bed, I would hear him say, "O Lord, if in thy wisdom thou hast ordained that my dear son shall have perished, do thou in infinite mercy strengthen me to bear up under it, that I may have grace given me. Thy will, O Lord, and not mine, be done."

The next day, at about eleven o'clock A.M., a messenger from town brought a telegram to father. He opened it, and it read as follows:

"———, December 3, 18—.
"EDWARD HORTON,

"Dreadful railroad accident; cars thrown off the bridge; eighty persons killed, and one hundred injured. We have one body of a man killed, but not burned. In the coat-pocket are papers bearing your name, being letters addressed to William Horton, Chicago; also grain and flour receipts, made to William Horton. Also, we have a satchel with his name on. We will express the body to you on receipt of your order by telegraph.

"———, Gen'l Sup't."

It seemed as though my father would sink into the ground; and had it not been for his true Christian fortitude he could not have endured the stroke.

But, like one of old, he exclaimed, "The Lord gave, and the Lord hath taken away; blessed be the name of the Lord." And, turning to me, said he, "Aspasia, we mourn not as those who have no hope. I shall soon go up yonder and meet him."

A message was at once sent to have the corpse of my dear brother forwarded by express, as suggested.

# CHAPTER X.

My father received a telegram from the superintendent, to the effect that the corpse of my brother William would arrive at three o'olock P.M. on Saturday.

At that time we were at the depot, with hosts of sympathizing friends.

John and James and their families, Kate and Elizabeth and their husbands, were all with us; and, as soon as the coffin was placed in the hearse, the church-bell commenced tolling, and continued until the procession arrived at the church where the funeral ceremonies were performed.

There were a great many people present. Mr. Shaw was so deeply affected by the sudden bereavement that he could not officiate; and the Rev. Mr. Clark, pastor of the Baptist church, kindly offered his services; and they were intensely solemn and impressive.

He dwelt at length upon the great loss the community had sustained by this sudden death; that the deceased was a young man of strict integrity, of remarkable judgment, an enterprising and public-spirited man, and, withal, a devoted and active Christian; and both the church and community had suffered an irreparable loss, and it was fitting that so large a congregation had assembled to express their sympathy for the relatives of the deceased, and particularly for the grief-stricken father; and also that they could, by thus bending around the bier,

10* (113)

find a momentary relief in shedding tears of sorrow over the remains of one so universally beloved.

A quartette choir stood at the head of the coffin, in front of the pulpit, and sang a funeral hymn; and I thought I had never heard them sing so well. I afterward remarked to father that it seemed to me as though William's spirit was aiding them; for he was a very fine musician, and I certainly never heard that choir sing so sweetly and in such perfect tune.

We were all broken down by this terrible affliction; but I dared not exhibit my emotions of sorrow in presence of my father, for it seemed as though he was completely crushed by his deep grief. And when, before God, at the family altar, he prayed that "this deep affliction might be sanctified to himself and his remaining children for their spiritual and everlasting good," the throbbings of his heart choked his utterance, and he exclaimed, "The Lord gave, and the Lord hath taken away; blessed be the name of the Lord." Then it was that I could fully realize the strength and power of the Christian's faith.

Time passed on, and my father's health seemed to fail. He mourned for William's death more as a child would at the loss of a parent in whom he trusted, than as a parent who had lost a child.

For my father was growing old, and not so vigorous as formerly, and he looked forward with no little anxiety to the time when he should become (if he lived) helpless, and, to use his own expression, useless, and would then be dependent upon William; that all his hopes for the future of this life centered in him.

It was a cold, dreary, and sad winter with us.

> "Lone minstrel of the pensive lyre,
>  Oh, let not grief attune thy lay;
> For sadness blights each holier fire,
>  And scatters gloom o'er all the way."

After the extreme cold of winter had passed, I persuaded father to accompany me on a visit to sister Elizabeth, where we spent two weeks, but not very pleasantly; for I regret to say that Elizabeth, unlike any other member of our family, was petulant and cross. She had a little boy, about a year and a half old, as bright and pretty a little fellow as I ever saw; and she would fly into a passion and cuff the "little brat" twenty times a day. She had a boy, of about ten years of age, that she took to bring up; and I thought he had a good deal better have never come up at all than to be "brought up" in her way. But she said she was going to learn him to "bear the yoke in his youth."

I really pitied her husband. He was a gentleman of superior business abilities, of very fine talents for public speaking; but she would never permit him to make a speech, or accept an office of honor and trust, either in town or church, if she could prevent it; she said "she didn't like to see people put themselves forward;" and although her husband had sufficient independence and self-respect not to conform to all of her foolish and wicked caprices, yet it was a very great annoyance and affliction to him, and also a great hindrance to his usefulness.

On his return home from the labors of the day, his brain racked till he was well-nigh exhausted, wearied and careworn, when of all times he needed, and ought to have received, the cordial sympathies of an affectionate wife, she would be more likely to meet him with a reprehend than otherwise; and although he would generally pay no attention to her, and appear not to hear her at all, and, catching up his precious little boy, play with him, yet occasionally he would lose his patience,—and then, my lady, look out; the fur would fly for a few moments; then all would be as still as it usually is immediately succeeding a violent storm, and for a few days all was serene and lovely.

Just before leaving for home, I ventured to read my sister a short lecture, and one which she did not altogether relish. Still, I felt it my duty; but, alas! she did not heed it; and she was compelled to mourn in sackcloth and ashes in after-years; for her husband died, leaving her poor, with children; and the neighbors, well knowing her treatment of him, did not manifest that regard and sympathy for her they otherwise would have done. And I have heard her many times utter deep regrets at the errors and follies of her married life.

Spring came, and Mr. Goodspeed began to grow impatient to be married; but I was not yet ready. I, one day, while conversing with father, remarked to him that I was not sure I really loved Mr. Goodspeed. I could not but feel as though there was something wrong with him. A casual acquaintance would not reveal anything wrong; but I thought I could detect a certain sort of something which I could not explain, which led me to fear he was not so good at heart as he would have me believe. My father inquired what indications I had to suspect that he was not honest. I replied, I could not tell; yet such impressions had been fastening themselves upon my mind from time to time, and I could not give any reasons that would be satisfactory to any one,—and, indeed, none whatever, except that an occasional unguarded expression in his conversation and his letters, and the general tone and spirit which seemed to underlie his whole life, had fastened the conviction on my mind that the substratum of his character was exceedingly porous, and that it needed to be broken up by the plowshare of grace before much real good could be expected from him.

I have heard my father say that when he went to look up land with a view of purchasing, if he found brakes and wintergreens growing, even but occasionally, among the grass, although by an extra dressing of some fertilizer the grass should appear plentiful, yet he would know the soil was wet and cold, and would require constant stimulating in order to produce a crop.

So also, when he found the sorrel and certain other weeds, he knew that the ground of itself was dry and barren, and could only be induced to yield a crop by tickling or teasing.

Experience teaches me that there is great similarity between the nature of mind and the nature of soil. There are fields which, of their own accord, will produce abundant crops of luxuriant grass every year, entirely free of noxious weeds. So there are hearts that are constantly full of holy emotions, and develop by every look and act the highest degree of virtue and moral honesty.

As my father returned from the village one day in the early part of June, I observed an appearance of melancholy that was unusual, and inquired the cause.

Seating himself in his arm-chair, he sat silent for some moments. At length he addressed me.

"Aspasia, we are ruined."

"How is that, father?" said I.

He replied, "You remember that a few days after your mother's funeral Mr. Wm. G. Hoxey came here to see me."

"Yes," said I; "and I remember how full of sympathy he appeared to be; and I thought then it was put on. I didn't believe it was genuine, but that he was actuated from selfish motives. Well, what of him?"

"Your suspicions were correct. But it is a very

great pity that you did not put me on my guard; for somehow it seems as though Providence has endowed you with more common sense and sagacity than all the rest of the family.

"Well, after he had commiserated me on account of my deep affliction, he said he was also in trouble which caused him deep distress; but, unlike my affliction, which no earthly friend could alleviate, his could be. I inquired what it was. He said he had become involved through some speculations, and his home was mortgaged to secure his creditors, and the time of redemption had about expired, and if sold would reduce himself and family to extreme poverty; and he desired to negotiate a loan of twenty thousand dollars for two years and a half, and in that time he could pay it; and that if Mr. Geo. B. Scott and myself would indorse the notes for him he could get the money; and that he had seen Mr. Scott, and he agreed to sign if I would. Without much reflection, I signed them. He then went to Esquire Scott and obtained his signature. And now, as you are aware, Mr. Scott is dead, his estate is declared insolvent, Hoxey has failed, and the notes are past due, and not a dollar has been paid, even the interest. And to-day I have been sued for twenty-eight thousand dollars; and it will take every dollar of property and money I have, and then not more than two-thirds pay the debt. O Lord, have mercy on us. Oh that my grief were thoroughly weighed, and my calamity laid in the balances together."

I was so choked with grief that I could not speak; and, after a few moments' silence, I heard him exclaim, in an under-tone, "Be still, and know that I am God."

I asked him if there was no possible escape. He replied, "None whatever."

After committing our ways unto the Lord, in our evening's devotions, we retired for the night, but not to sleep.

Some of my readers may have experienced the cold blasts of the storms of adversity. Such can appreciate the terrible agony of mind we felt that long and wearisome night. At length the morning dawned, and all was beautiful without, but in striking contrast with our wounded spirits.

There were times when it seemed as though I must curse God and die; but then I would remember the cross of Christ, and his teachings: "If ye endure not chastisement, then are ye not sons." And, to be a child of God and an heir with Christ, I must meekly submit to his providences.

After breakfast we rode to the village, and broke the unwelcome news to Kate and Mr. Shaw; and they too were filled with sorrow. Mr. Shaw and my father went to consult Esquire Hicks, a celebrated lawyer. He said there was no escape; the debt would have to be paid, so far as father's property would go toward paying it. My father then called on the holder of the notes, and said to him that if he would exercise leniency toward himself and daughter, who were now in a day reduced to poverty, he would turn over everything he had, and execute papers at once and save time and expense at law. To this the gentleman gladly assented. It was done; and within one month we were homeless and penniless.

I had written full particulars to Mr. Goodspeed, and received a reply urging me to marry him now. I declined for the present; for my father needed me more than ever.

Soon the news of my father's misfortunes spread over the town, and the people all seemed to sympathize with

us; and good old Jane Fisher circulated a subscription-
paper to raise money for father. As for me, she said, I
could take care of myself; and so I could.

The result was, a collection of three thousand dollars,
conditioned that it be invested in seven-thirty government bonds and placed on special deposit with the selectmen of the town, and that they should pay over the interest to my father each year semi-annually as it matured,
to be expended by him for his board.

As soon as this was all accomplished, Jane came into
Mr. Shaw's; for father and I were stopping there a few
days till I could obtain employment.

She met us all in her usual don't-care sort of style,
and, said she, " Mr. Horton, I have been young, and now
am old, and yet I have never seen the righteous forsaken,
nor his seed begging bread. Read that, Mr. Horton,"
handing him a paper, "and see if there isn't a God in
Israel."

My father commenced to read it.

"Oh," said she "read it aloud, so all can hear it; for
may-be they won't like it."

My father read it, as follows :

"July —, 18—.

"EDWARD HORTON, ESQ.

"MY DEAR SIR:—You have been a life-long resident of
this town. You have always been in affluent circumstances, which enabled you to act the emotions of your
soul and freely contribute to all charitable objects. You
have ever been actuated, in all your dealings with the
people of this and the neighboring towns, by principles
of honor and strict integrity; you have always exhibited
a high degree of public spirit, and so deported yourself as
to merit and command the admiration and esteem of all
the people; and it is to show the great degree of respect

they entertain for you, and their sympathy that you are called to wade through the deep waters of adversity, that I am commissioned to hand you this letter, and in it say to you that, by contributions from nearly every voter in this town, three thousand dollars in seven-thirty government bonds have been purchased and placed in the hands of the selectmen, to be kept so long as you shall live; and the interest shall be paid to you by the chairman of the board, semi-annually, on the 15th of July and January of each year, and at your death it shall revert to the original donors.

> "With eminent expressions of our high esteem,
> "I am yours respectfully,
> "For the donors,
> "SAML. HAYNES,
> "*Chairman of Selectmen.*"

My father was so deeply moved by this manifestation of regard that it was with difficulty that he could read it through; and, upon concluding it, we all enjoyed a good hearty crying, in which Jane participated.

At Jane's suggestion, it was concluded to have father live with Mr. Shaw. The interest would just about pay his board.

God in his providence having in so mysterious a manner provided for my father, I now cast about in earnest for something to do to support myself. I applied for a school in a neighboring town; and, by some means, Mr. Goodspeed heard of it, as also did Rose (Mrs. Shepherd), and Mr. Goodspeed came at once to visit me, and brought a letter from Rose, insisting that I must not defer marriage any longer, and that she craved the privilege of giving me a wedding-party on my arriving in the city.

Mr. Goodspeed now resumed his suit, and his arguments, based upon my ill fortune, I confess were forcible; and the result was that, after considering it, and praying over it for a day or two, I finally yielded; and said I, "Morgan Goodspeed, do you offer me your heart and hand without reserve, and prompted only by the purest emotions of love?"

"I certainly do," he replied; "and I think my constancy of purpose, as evinced during the past three years, is a sufficient guarantee of my sincerity."

"It is," I replied; "and I accept you."

The day for the wedding was decided upon, and that the ceremony should be performed in our church, and my brother-in-law, Mr. Shaw, should officiate.

Mr. Goodspeed returned home, and I hastened my preparations for the wedding, which was to take place two weeks from the Sabbath following.

# CHAPTER XI

"They tell me the vision of bliss that is glinting,
  My heart's star of promise, in gloom will decline,
· And the fair scene that Fancy, the fairy, is tinting,
  Will lose all its sunny glow ere it is mine.

"Oh, if Love and Life be but a fairy illusion,
  And the cold future bright but in Fancy's young eye,
Still let me live in the dreamy delusion,
  And, true and unchanging, hope on till I die."

THE two weeks in which I had to prepare for the wedding passed swiftly by; and on the Friday previous, Mr. Goodspeed arrived.

Sabbath morning at last came,—a beautiful morning, the 9th day of August, 18—. I thought I never saw the sun shine forth with greater brilliancy and splendor; and, in my meditations, a strange sensation came over me. I thought over the scenes of my early life, of the pleasures of my childhood days, of the happy hours at home, "the dear old home," of a father's and mother's counsel and prayers, of the precious privileges which it had pleased a kind Providence to grant me; and I realized that this day I was to part with youth forever, and enter upon womanhood; and, however much pleasure and happiness I anticipated in view of my marriage, as my mind reverted to the pleasures of former days I could but feel, "Oh that I were a girl again!" But then, I thought, to be always a girl is not answering the highest purpose and aim for which I was designed; and it is

(123)

the part of a Christian philosopher to enjoy life as it passes, and the highest degree of happiness in this life can only be attained by performing acts of charity and love fully commensurate to the age and ability of the individual.

Casting aside the reminiscences of former days, its pleasures and pains, its joys and its sorrows, its prosperity and its adversity, I looked forward with bright anticipations to the full fruition of earthly happiness as the result of my married life.

Time came for church-service. Arriving at church, we found the congregation assembled and in waiting.

We were all seated by Mr. Shaw in his pew. Taking his place in his pulpit, the choir sang a voluntary, and soon services commenced.

Mr. Shaw preached from the text, "Love one another," and I could but think he was reading a lecture to Mr. Goodspeed and myself; and if I didn't observe sly glances between him and Kate, then I am mistaken. It may be that, owing to my trepidation, it was simply my imaginings. Be that as it may, I confess that I was neither very highly entertained nor instructed by the preaching that day, nor did I relish my position as being an exhibition; for I felt that I was gazed upon by the entire congregation.

After sermon, the marriage ceremony was performed. The choir sang a lovely anthem, the benediction was pronounced, and the congregation retired.

But my friends were so earnest to give me a parting salutation, as they said, "possibly for the last time," that it was with difficulty that we could crowd our way out of the house; and good old Jane Fisher—bless her soul!—came to me with her eyes almost blinded with tears, and said she, "Aspasia, you know how much I thought of your mother, and you look just exactly like her, and you don't know how sorry I am to see that you are about to leave us forever. God bless you! Remember me in your prayers;" and, putting her mouth close to my ear, she whispered, "Are you going to live in Boston? and shall you keep house, or board? Folks will ask me, and I want to tell it just as it is."

I replied, " I could not yet say, but as soon as it was determined, I would endeavor to write her."

This seemed to satisfy her craving inquisitiveness, and we were all soon seated in the carriage, and on the way home.

My husband and myself retired to our room; I threw myself into a chair, and buried my face in my handkerchief, and cried like a child. My husband sat silent. As soon as I recovered from my fit of sadness, I sprang to him, and, throwing my arms about his neck, said I, "Morgan Goodspeed, my husband, I love you. It was not simply that I am married that caused this sadness to come over me, but it was because I must now bid adieu forever to all my dear friends who have been so very kind to my parents and myself at all times, in adversity as well as prosperity, and that I must now turn from the scenes of my childhood, and enter upon the realities of life. And, while I cannot bury the past in oblivion, I cannot but be sensible of the crushing weight of the responsibilities of the future which I am to bear. And, oh, I fear that I shall not prove equal to the task; and I beg—beg? no, I claim—your manly forbearance and charity, pledging you, before my God, that, so long as life lasts, I will ever and at all times prove myself your loving and devoted wife."

He clasped me to his bosom, and for a moment we were silent; at last he spoke, as follows:

" We will not deplore, then, the days that are past ;
   The gloom of misfortune is over them cast ;
   They were lengthened by sorrow, and sullied by care ;
   Their griefs were too many, their joys were too rare ;
   Yet now, that their shadows are on us no more,
   Let us welcome the prospect that brightens before.

"Oh let us no longer, then, vainly lament
   Over scenes that have faded, or days that are spent;
   But, by faith unforsaken, unawed by mischance,
   On hope's waving banner still fixed be our glance;
   And, should fortune prove cruel and false to the last,
   Let us look to the future and not to the past."

  " Very well," said I, "but,

"As we look back through life in our moments of sadness,
   How few and how brief are its gleamings of gladness;
   Yet we find, midst the gloom that our pathway o'ershaded,
   A few spots of sunshine,—a few flowers unfaded ;—
   And memory still hoards, as her richest of treasures,
   Some moments of rapture,—some exquisite pleasures."

Monday came, and sister Kate and myself commenced, packing the large Saratoga trunk, which, by some strange freak of fortune, had fallen to me.

I say fortune, and indeed it was ; for I could not have provided myself with one at this time, for lack of money.

Tuesday morning came, and, bidding the dear ones "good-by," we were safe on board the cars for the city that was to be my future home.

We arrived in Boston at half-past four P.M. of that day, "safe and sound ;" and I was overjoyed and astounded to find my old friend Rose, and her husband and some twenty or thirty other gentlemen, and as many ladies, in waiting at the depot to welcome us on our arrival, and escort us to Mrs. Shepherd's mansion.

I afterward learned from my husband that, according
to agreement, he telegraphed Mrs. Shepherd in the morning when he expected to arrive, and said nothing to me,
preferring to take me by surprise, to see how I should
appear under circumstances so calculated to embarrass
almost any lady.

"Well," said I, "how did I appear ?"

"Splendidly," he replied.

"Thank you, my dear," said I. "I hope I may always
please you, and receive in return the devotion of your
noble heart."

Being wearied with my day's ride, and the excitement
consequent upon the circumstances which I have nar-
rated, I retired to rest early.

I passed the following day (Wednesday) very pleasantly with Mrs. Shepherd; and that evening we all attended the church social-meeting, and it was indeed a
precious season. I noticed (or at least I thought I did)
that my husband was considerably affected; which gave
me great encouragement. I had vowed to God never
to cease my prayers nor my pleadings for and with
him. For however much I loved him, and however
intense was his love for me, I could not feel safe and
secure in his pledges unless I had the fullest assurance
that he had been renewed in the spirit of his mind by
the power and grace of God. I had learned that all the
resolutions of a soul unsanctified by grace were weak
and unreliable, and, however good the moral intentions
were, in the day of extreme temptation that soul would
fall away; and therefore my only safety for the future
of my life rested in the results of the operation of
God's Spirit upon my dear husband's heart. I was determined to perform my duty at the throne of grace in
his behalf; well knowing that if I did the Holy Spirit

would surely manifest His presence,—which would result either in his conversion or tend to harden him in sin. If the former, the glory would be God's; if the latter, he would have to "bear his own iniquity," and I should "save my own soul."

And here I will say to my young readers, as you are coming up the steep and rugged paths of life, you will find nothing that will soften down the asperities of the way like a well-grounded hope in Christ. You may start out in your own strength with the best resolves; but you will meet here and there, as you clamber over the cliffs, the fiery darts of temptation hurled against you with such rapidity and force that you will not be able to maintain your standing in the road, or to pursue your journey by your own strength, skill, or nerve. You will then find that you need the aid of one stronger than yourself; and Jesus is that one. He said, "My strength is sufficient for thee." He "has trodden the wine-press of the wrath of God alone," "when there was none to help," and knows full well how to pity poor, weak, fallen humanity. Therefore it is that "He ever liveth to make intercession for us, with groanings which cannot be uttered."

The friends of Mrs. Shepherd were anxious she should give my wedding party on Wednesday evening; but she declined. Both herself and husband were devoted Christians; and, although they enjoyed the innocent pleasures of life to a degree exceeded by none, and were possessed of ample wealth to afford them all the luxuries which their souls might crave, yet they squared their whole life by the principles of Christ's teachings, and were always happy.

Thursday evening came, and with it my wedding-party at Mrs. Shepherd's.

The elegant parlors and reception-rooms were thrown

open to the brilliant party assembled, and the élite of the
city, to the number of over four hundred, were present.
All that wealth could do was done to render the party a
brilliant one; the ladies fairly sparkled with diamonds.
The evening passed off very pleasantly; I formed many
new acquaintances, some of whom afterward became
valuable friends.

Late in the evening dancing commenced, and I received
several invitations to dance, all of which I was compelled
to decline, from the simple reason that I did not know
how. One gentleman, a Mr. Howard, who very politely
invited me to dance with him, and received my oft-re-
peated excuse, felt himself called upon to discuss the
dancing question; and, expressing his surprise that a lady
who occupied so exalted a position in society as myself
should not understand the dance, inquired whether I
thought it wrong to dance. I replied that, so far as the
simple act of dancing, or jumping up and down, was concerned, there was nothing sinful or immoral; but I thought
it a very foolish amusement, and one that led to immoral
practices, the tendency of which was deleterious to society. True, it did not produce this effect upon all who
participated in it, nor upon a majority, for, if it did, society would indeed be in a pitiable condition; but for a
young gentleman or lady to engage in it under all circumstances, when opportunity offered, it certainly would require a heroic mind to resist the evil influences engen-
dered by such associations; therefore it was that I dis-
approved of it, and, aside from that, I thought it a very
foolish amusement; and that if the time spent by ladies
and gentlemen in dancing could be occupied in conversation upon subjects that were elevating to the mind, I felt
sure its influence in moulding society for good would be
felt and appreciated.

I begged the gentleman's pardon for so fully expressing my views, but since he had, as he supposed, "flanked my battery," I was compelled either to resist or retreat: the latter I never do, at least not until I have exhausted my means of defense. He would, therefore, please excuse me without offense; which he very pleasantly assured me he did, remarking, "I shall think of what you have said, for I am inclined to respect your judgment."

At a late hour the party broke up, and the guests each gave us a hearty parting salutation as they left.

Thus ended the introduction of Mr. and Mrs. Good-speed to the élite of Boston society.

We spent the remainder of the week, and until the Monday following, at Mr. and Mrs. Shepherd's, and passed the time pleasantly in reminiscences of former days and prognostications of the future; but, although in my marriage everything was as propitious as heart could wish, still, when left to my own reflections, a certain sort of sadness came over me at the thought that I had lived out one period of my life, and that, too, a very important one, and had, so far as I could discover, fallen far short of my privileges in the accomplishment of the highest good for which I was born.

Sabbath came, and with it we all repaired to church; and after the voluntary on the grand old organ, by one of the best performers I ever had the pleasure of listening to, the venerable divine arose, and read the following hymn:

> " Blest be the tie that binds
> Our hearts in Christian love."

The pastor requested that the whole congregation, or all who could, should join in singing this old and familiar hymn. I really do not know that my recent marriage had

anything to do with the reading of that hymn, but I confess I could not help feeling that it had. The sermon,
which, by the way, exhibited a high order of talent in the
writer, was upon the establishment of the kingdom of
Jesus Christ upon the earth.

The theory advanced by the venerable divine was, that
the thousand years of the millennium would be three hundred and sixty-five thousand years as we reckon time,
"for a thousand years are with God as one day ;" "and
that during that period Jesus would reign as king in person upon the earth, and peace and righteousness cover
the earth as waters do the great deep;" "that death from
disease would gradually decrease until no such thing
would be known" (and here I said to myself, "What
will become of doctors?"); "and that death by violence
would not occur at all : the earth will rapidly return to
its original estate of beauty, purity, and perfection, and
the savage beasts lose their ferocity, and there will be
a literal fulfillment of the prophecy, 'The lion shall lie
down, etc.;' and, at the end of this period, death will be
banished from the earth, and the whole earth will be
made as beautiful as the garden of Eden when God
looked upon it at the first, and saw that it was very good.
And it will be peopled with an immortal race of beings ;
all who have previously died, trusting in Christ, shall rise
to newness of life, and, with all who are then living, will
put on immortality ; and, as stated in the 24th verse of the
15th chapter of 2d Corinthians, Jesus will then deliver up
the kingdom, as an interceding priest, to God, even the
Father God, and then will be fulfilled the vision of the
relation of a new heaven and a new earth, for the first
heaven (meaning the spirit-world, where the souls of the
saints repose until the final judgment) and the first earth
(referring to this sin-cursed earth as it now appears) were

passed away; then will also be fulfilled that which was spoken by Jesus, 'The meek shall inherit the earth.' Jesus will then appear all-glorious, exalted by God to be a King and a Prince forever; God will triumph over the works of Satan, the earth will be purified and restored as before the fall, and man redeemed from sin, and from under the curse of the law, made pure and holy, as at the first, and the earth his everlasting home with Jesus his King."

The sermon was intensely interesting throughout its entire delivery.

I would like to give a fuller synopsis of the discourse, with his references, had I time.

I accept the theory of a purified and redeemed earth as the future eternal heaven with pleasure, and I fancy that if this doctrine were more generally preached, its tendency would be to remove a great deal of skepticism from the minds of men; for we are all so constituted that it is difficult to believe in a heaven without a locality, quite as difficult as to believe in a God without a person.

Why is it that the heathen in all ages have had, and still have, their images of wood and stone? It is simply because they represent their ideal of God, or gods, not that they really are gods, but the ideal of God.

Thus it was that Christ the Lord God came from heaven in the person of Jesus, that he might satisfy this demand of man for a perfect intelligence, on whom man could look, knowing him as God.

"And thus he was lifted up as the brazen serpent was lifted up in the wilderness, that all who looked might live."

On returning from church, Mr. Shepherd inquired of me what I thought of the sermon. I replied that I was highly entertained and instructed; the ideas advanced might be, and probably were, new to many, but they were so forcibly presented, and so clearly substantiated by Bible texts, and all harmonized so perfectly with my preconceived views of heaven as a locality, and the soul's want of a theory of this sort, based upon the Bible, reason, and sound judgment, that I most heartily indorsed them. And one sublime thought, not adverted to by the speaker, but which naturally grew out of the sermon, and struck me with great force, and in the consideration of which the mind becomes completely overwhelmed, is the degree of perfection which men will attain in the arts and sciences during those three hundred and sixty five thousand years spoken of by the preacher.

What wonderful advancement in knowledge has been made by man during the last half century! Then all travel was by the slow coach; day after day and night after night, jolting along the highway, and but one short journey could be made in a twelvemonth, by reason of the time, expense, and fatigue consequent upon the mode of conveyance.

And by water it was subjecting one's self to the monotonous swell of the waves, being slowly urged forward by heaven's gentle breezes, or, betimes, driven with violence before the storm.

Now two weeks is sufficient in which to cross the broad Atlantic in a floating palace, propelled by the mighty unseen force of steam.

And we can compass a continent in a single week in a palace on wheels, drawn by the iron horse.

And, so far as time, the fatigue and expense of travel, and written correspondence are concerned, friends who are to-day separated by thousands of miles are neighbors close at hand, as compared with the times and circumstances of fifty years ago.

And being able, as we are, to bridle that mysterious, unseen force we call electricity, and drive it by any route we choose, we can, by its aid, send a message, as quick as thought, from one end of the earth to the other, or around the world; and thus men who are separated as wide as the world talk to each other as neighbors.

Turn over the pages of the past, one, two, three, four hundred years, and contrast the condition of the world then with the present. Then "darkness covered the earth, and gross darkness the people;" but now the light of God's truth shines (though dimly) in the minds and hearts of men; and thus the mind, directed by Bible-teachings, intelligently searching for God, that great, all-powerful, unseen force, has become by degrees, and in a measure, enlightened, and able to develop and apply to practical use wonderful inventions in the arts and sciences, even to count the stars all by name, and in all knowledge to so far excel his fellow of the past, that could one of the sleepers of a hundred years ago now step out upon earth and witness the progress of this age, he would, in his astonishment, be inclined to exclaim, "Indeed, ye are gods, and not men."

Now, then, in view of the unlimited growth of mind, and reasoning from analogy, what a glorious world will this be a hundred thousand years hence, or, if that is too far a stretch of the mind, how glorious will the world become one thousand years hence! The man of intelligence of this day will be but a mere pigmy, as compared with him who shall stand upon the same ground a hundred thousand years hence; and I believe that the souls of all those who have died, and those who will die, will, in their advancement, keep pace with the increase of knowledge among men on the earth, and thus be fitted in all things, at the great resurrection, for associating with the countless millions of earth's inhabitants when the "kingdom shall be given up to God the Father, and Jesus Christ shall take to himself his almighty power and reign."

"Well," replied Mr. Shepherd, "I was myself greatly interested in the sermon, but, not being so well prepared to accept the doctrines and theories advanced as you were, I did not so fully appreciate them, but I do now, and I most sincerely thank you for your elucidation of the subject."

# CHAPTER XII.

On Monday we left our friends, Mr. and Mrs. Shepherd, and commenced boarding, having obtained a very pleasant suite of rooms, which my husband furnished in elegant style.

And as I look back over my married life, I find the days spent in those rooms among my happiest.

We took a pew in Dr. Eddy's church, and I united with the church by letter; and, while it was a happy thought that in the city of my new home I found, through the channels of religion, the same congeniality that I had ever enjoyed at my old home, yet it was a painful thought that my dear husband, him whom I had taken as the partner of my life, the sharer of my joys and sorrows, could not join with me in communing with Jesus.

Soon after uniting with the church I was urged to teach in the Sabbath-school. My husband was at first inclined to object, for he said he was so intensely occupied in his business during the week that he desired my company on the Sabbath; but I persuaded him, and he gave his consent.

I took charge of a large class of young ladies: several, however, were not very young, in fact, some were older even than myself. I soon found many of them so intelligent that it required pretty close study on my part, during my leisure hours, to fit myself for the duties of the Sabbath. And my husband would, at such times, up-

( 136 )

braid me, and urge me to abandon the class, to which I replied, "Never. I never abandon anything I undertake. 'I must be about my Master's business.' If I can do any good, you certainly are willing that I may. I am sure you would delight to have it said that your wife is one of the leading ladies in the church, would you not?" At the same time, throwing my arms about his neck, I gave him a good, hearty kiss.

I used that argument with him to stimulate generous impulses, through his pride; and I succeeded, for he replied:

"I do not like to see you toiling so hard for nothing; but, if it affords you any pleasure, I have no objection."

And many an evening thereafter, while preparing myself for the discussion of a difficult theme, he would volunteer his assistance in my researches, until he became interested to such an extent that he was almost induced to become a member of a gentleman's class himself; but, alas! how difficult it is for men, whose minds are absorbed in the things of this life, to bring themselves to a practical consideration of those things which are of vastly greater importance to them than all earthly treasures!

I am not opposed to wealth, far from it, or to that diligence which maketh rich. The possession of wealth need not of necessity encumber a person's soul; but that it does so, in very many cases, cannot be denied, while, at the same time, there are those who are made stewards of God's bounties, who glorify God with their substance; they are ever on the alert to search out the poor and distressed and alleviate their wants. These are the salt of the earth; and were it not for the seasoning such men impart, society would be in a deplorable condition.

Weeks and months passed away. One year had about expired,—for which we engaged board,—and I was expecting soon to commence housekeeping, when I was taken very ill; and, aside from my physical suffering, I grieved at being confined to my room, on account of my husband's anxiety to move into his new house, just furnished and ready; for he was anticipating great pleasure (as he said) "at commencing to live."

Finding that I was not likely to recover rapidly from my illness, I was, in a few weeks, removed carefully to our new house; and all that a loving husband and attentive servants and the aid of friends could do was done to render me comfortable and hasten my recovery.

It was not long thereafter that I presented my husband his first-born, a beautiful boy.

So soon as I was able to ride we took him to the font, before the altar, and dedicated him to God in baptism. We named him for my lost brother William.

Oh, how many hours have I sat and anxiously watched the countenance of that little angel as he lay in the basket-cradle, like some waif, the lost jewel of the Great King, and tried to divine from the lineaments of the beautiful face the character of that immortal mind, which was comparatively dormant, and only developed itself unconsciously as the wants of nature demanded.

My husband now became more attached to home than ever before; his darling boy seemed the idol of his heart, and, as he grew in stature, so he also grew in his father's affections.

Time passed on, and I presented my husband with two daughters, perfect in body and mind, for which we sincerely thanked a kind Providence. We named the eldest Rose, in memory of my dearest friend, and the youngest Bell, for one who, by her virtues, contributed to the happiness of my social life in youth.

Our boy William had come to be ten years of age,

our eldest daughter, Rose, eight, and Bell six years of age; and they had all been thoroughly instructed from the Bible from the time they could lisp the name of Jesus; and every Sabbath found them in their classes at the Sabbath-school.

About this time I observed that my dear husband did not seem to respect my religious views as much as formerly, and needlessly absented himself from church, offering some frivolous excuse; all of which pained me deeply. He was kind to me in all other respects. Possessed, as he was, of ample means, and carrying on a very profitable business, I was not allowed to feel the want of anything, neither were the children, and he freely gave me money to appropriate for charitable objects as I saw fit.

And in my reflections upon my dear husband's course of life, I could but think that he was in the same sad case as the young man spoken of by Christ. "One thing thou lackest." And I prayed more fervently for him than ever. In the morning, after he had left for his business, and at night, previous to his return, I would gather my dear children about me, and, all kneeling before God, I would pour out my soul's earnest desire that my children might be carried like lambs in Christ's bosom, and be preserved from the temptations and snares of this life. Then, oh, then it was that I felt the need of a sympathizing heart, to go with me to the mercy-seat.

And bidding the children to go about their plays, I would agonize in behalf of my dear husband, determined never to cease my pleadings until I should be permitted to see the answer to my supplications.

Time passed on, and my husband, from neglecting one duty after another, also began to neglect his family; and, notwithstanding my earnest entreaties to the contrary, he would frequent the club-room, returning at a late hour of the night, his clothing scented with the noxious fumes of tobacco, and occasionally I detected the odor of ardent spirits.

I always sat up for him. Never, I think, in a single instance, did I retire until his return. This he did not like, and urged me to retire at a seasonable hour; but I peremptorily declined, giving as my reason that his welfare, temporal and spiritual, was as dear to me as my own soul, and I could not, and would not, retire to rest any night until I knew he was safe.

I never upbraided him, but I would do all in my power each night, on his return, to render him comfortable and happy.

I was finally taken violently sick with fever, which soon assumed the typhoid form, and for one week I was delirious. During that time my husband (as I afterward learned) did not leave my bedside for an hour at a time, day nor night. He was very much alarmed lest I should not recover. And when I had so far rallied as to be able to converse with him, oh, what deep regrets did he express at his course of life during the years previous, and with what earnestness did he beg my pardon for his neglect!

I drew him to my pillow, and, with one of my warmest kisses, said I, "My dear husband, you are too good to cruelly neglect your family, unless you give yourself up to the influence of wicked persons. Oh, that you would give your heart to Jesus, to be wholly influenced by his Spirit! then there would be no danger; but you cannot keep yourself."

"Yes, I can," he replied, "and I shall never again treat you so ill." And he wept like a child.

"Alas!" said I to myself, "how little he knows of the frailty of man."

I was now so far recovered that my children (precious souls) were permitted to be about, and upon my bed. It was a great blessing that I could thus again enjoy them, and listen to their hearty congratulations upon my recovery.

I continued to grow better each day gradually, until, in the course of two months, I had regained my usual strength. My friends, Mr. and Mrs. Shepherd, were very solicitous as to the result of my severe sickness, and were untiring in their efforts to alleviate my sufferings and promote my speedy recovery. Many friends in the church and out of it were also attentive to me.

Upon riding to Mrs. Shepherd's (my first after my sickness), it seemed as though I was a new creature, or else I was in a new and beautiful world.

Have any of my readers ever been brought low by sickness, and confined for weeks by a burning fever, which well-nigh exhausted the system?

If so, upon going out into the world again, how new everything appears! one seems to look with new and clearer eyes; and every person you meet seems a friend. What the philosophy of this is I do not undertake to say; but this was my experience, and I doubt not it is that of others.

I suppose it is accounted for, in part, from the fact that during a long confinement the mind is divested of all perplexing cares or vexatious problems, and reasons with itself, and to a very great extent (in some more than others) divests itself of selfishness, and views humanity from the broad base of neighborly or brotherly affection.

Again; by being brought low in sickness, thus rendered helpless, and wholly dependent upon others, the individual comes to realize his weakness and dependence upon his fellow-man; and consequently his first associations with the world will be characterized by love.

Nothing but a consciousness of our weakness and personal inability, whether mental or physical, will ever bring us into such a condition of humility as to cause us to appreciate either God or our fellows; and, indeed, this sort of affliction (sickness) is absolutely essential to some people, to render them even endurable as neighbors.

I once knew a lady who was violent in her denunciations of all her acquaintances, proud, arrogant, and defiant, when she had enjoyed health for months; but, after being brought low in sickness (as she was many times), she was kind, soft-tempered, and quite lovable; all of which would wear off as she regained her strength and vigor, until it was the oft-expressed wish that "Mrs. Scott would have the fever again."

For several months after my recovery my husband remained firm in his promises of faithfulness to his family, and, with our three lovely children about us, we enjoyed a happy, happy home.

But, alas! how delicate and frail is the rose of earth's pleasure! In an hour it withers, droops, and dies.

God had raised me up from the very threshold of the grave, to lead me through the deep waters of trouble and adversity, to test my faith still stronger, and thus fit me for greater usefulness in this life, and a more exalted state in the future life of the soul.

# CHAPTER XIII.

My mind has been so deeply absorbed in my own affairs, and in the affairs of my precious family, that I have neglected to chronicle events that have transpired relating more especially to other friends.

Just previous to my severe sickness, taking my children with me, I visited my friends at my native town. By this time sister Kate's children had grown up around her like the fair, fresh, and healthy shoots under the shade, and by the aid of the life-giving principles of the noble parent-tree from which they sprang.

And although I thought my children were good (and they were), yet, when brought side by side with Kate's, I could but note the contrast. And I remarked to her that I believed my children were as good as they could be, and hers were good because they could not be otherwise. The difference in the temperaments of the two families was striking, and this was the cause of the difference in the conduct of the children: education was not at fault in either case.

I found my father quite feeble; for, although he was borne up under his trials by the Christian's hope, yet there was a conflict of mind constantly going on that impaired greatly the vigor of his physical system; and I was pained to note, while there, a gradual weakness coming upon him, and I could but think that he had not long to live.

( 143 )

An affair occurred in connection with the church while I was there, which I will relate, simply to show the faculty possessed by the Rev. Mr. Shaw, my brother-in-law, to heal dissensions in his church and between members, and preserve peace, and at the same time endear himself more than ever to his people.

As a wounded bird flutters in its agony, fearful of all about it, and tries to escape even from the hand of one who would bind up its wound and protect it from harm, so it was with the lady member of Mr. Shaw's church who was wounded by the darts of evil-minded sisters in the church; but, as the sequel will show, her faith was stronger than her fears, and, through the skill and management of her pastor, her usefulness was not in the least impaired.

The circumstances of the case were as follows:

A most excellent lady, by the name of Johnson, a member of Mr. Shaw's church, had taken a very active part in all church enterprises. If, for instance, there was to be a church fair, Mrs. Johnson was the lady who would first move in the matter, and by her talents and energy, and remarkable executive ability, it was always sure to succeed, and that, too, profitably. So with any and all affairs in connection with the church, until it came to this,—that before any undertaking was commenced it was conceded necessary that it should receive Mrs. Johnson's indorsement in order to insure success.

And certain evil-minded ladies in the church had become very jealous of Mrs. Johnson's increasing popularity, and sought to find something against her, to accuse her before the church, "to humble her," as they said. They could find nothing immoral in her character, and she never committed a mistake in her management of the several societies of which she was the presiding officer.

Three of these ladies, viz., Mrs. Wood, Mrs. Smith, and
Mrs. White, called on the pastor to enter a complaint,
saying Mrs. Johnson ought to be restrained from putting
herself forward so much, for the reason that her husband
was not a member of the church. They said it didn't
look well to them to see a lady, whose husband was not a
church-member, to be making herself quite so officious,
and they hoped Mr. Shaw would at once call upon Mrs.
Johnson and talk with her about it, and get her to resign.

"Resign what?" inquired Mr. Shaw.

"Why," said they, "resign her offices. She is the
President of the Sewing Society, President of the Ladies'
Relief Society, and President of the Ladies' Washing-
tonian Society."

"Well," said Mr. Shaw, "suppose she would resign
all those offices, whom could you get to take her place?
If I am going to see her and make your proposition, she
would first inquire who would accept those offices. For
I am sure she would be glad to resign if she knew the
duties of each office would be properly attended to."

"Resign!" said they: "we are surprised."

"Can't help that," replied Mr. Shaw. "I know Mrs.
Johnson so well, that I am sure she would be glad to be
relieved, if she knew the positions would be well filled."

To this they expressed great astonishment. "For,"
said Mrs. Wood, "I can't understand why any one should
wish to resign so respectable a position."

Mr. Shaw replied that it was not every respectable
position that made the occupant respectable, or even respected; but a respectable person would dignify and
render respectable any position he might be called to
occupy.

13

"And now, ladies, please allow me to say that a sister in the church, whom I shall not name, has called on me and informed me that Mrs. Johnson has heard that something of this sort is going on, and she is feeling very badly about it. She says she has done all she could for the church with no selfish motives, and thinks I ought to use my influence to crush out the feeling against her, and I thought of calling on her this afternoon; but, from what I have learned of her feelings, I thought it best to let her alone a few days.

" But now you have one proposition for me to make to Mrs. Johnson, viz., that she resign her presidencies. Whom would you suggest as her successor?"

" Well," said Mrs. White, " I don't believe any one lady ought to think of filling all those offices."

" Neither do I," said Mrs. Smith; "and I would suggest Mrs. White as President of the Sewing Society."

" Thank you," said Mrs. White: " I didn't think of such a thing. But I will suggest Mrs. Wood as President of the Ladies' Relief Society."

" Thank you," said Mrs. Wood: " I really ought to consult my husband before I accept it. And I would suggest Mrs. Smith as President of the Washingtonian Society."

" Well, ladies," said Mr. Shaw, " you have been so kind as to nominate three most excellent persons to succeed Mrs. Johnson in case she resigns, and persons of all others that I believe she would choose herself, and I have very little doubt but she will resign if asked to. But the complaint you urge I do not quite see the force of. You say your objection to Mrs. Johnson is chiefly because her husband is not a member of the church. Now, my opinion is, that is the very reason why she should be sustained in holding those offices. For, in the first place, every one concedes that Mr. Johnson is one of the best men in the town."

"Why, Mr. Shaw!" said they. "You a minister, and yet say that a man who is not a member of the church is one of the best men in the town."

"Yes, most assuredly I do," replied Mr. Shaw. "Is there any brother in our church who attends meetings more regularly than Mr. Johnson, or who pays more devout attention to the preaching than he, or one who contributes more liberally for the support of the church than he?"

"No," said Mrs. White; "that is all very true; but, then, you know that a man may do all these and yet not be a Christian."

"Very true," replied Mr. Shaw. "But is there any man in this town who contributes more liberally to alleviate the poor in their distresses than does he, or one who is more attentive and kind to the sick of the neighborhood? And did you ever hear a person say that there were any indications of dishonesty in his dealings with others?"

"No," said Mrs. Smith; "but this moral way of living does not constitute a man a Christian."

"Well," said Mr. Shaw, "will not a sincere Christian do just as Mr. Johnson does?"

"Well, yes," said Mrs. Wood; "but they will do it from a pure motive."

"How do you know that Mr. Johnson is not actuated from the purest of motives? Have you ever looked into a man's heart, so as to be able to judge correctly of the motive which prompts his acts? Christ said (not by their motives, but), By their fruits ye shall know them. And as the fruits of the Christian's life, he enumerates these very duties which you confess Mr. Johnson performs. Therefore, what right have you or I to say that Mr. Johnson is not a Christian?

" We hear of no neighborhood-quarrels he is engaged in, while, as you may be aware, we have church-members who are continually in trouble with their neighbors. I should be rejoiced could Mr. Johnson see it his duty, as well as privilege, to unite with the church, for he would be a very efficient member, and, I doubt not, would stimulate others to a higher degree of piety; but you should understand, ladies, that the church never saves a soul, while the united prayers of God's people may and do prevail with God to save men; but the simple fact of subscribing to our creed, and having one's name entered on the roll of the church, is of itself of no avail for our salvation; that does not constitute a Christian, by any means; but, on the contrary, if we, before the world, put on the garments of righteousness, and then live as sinners live, and even worse than some sinners do, we shall be like the foolish virgins who had no oil in their lamps.

" Christ says, 'Not every one that saith unto me, Lord, Lord, have we not eaten and drunk in thy name, etc., shall inherit the kingdom of heaven, but he that *doeth* the will of my Father.'"

The ladies looked with astonishment at Mr. Shaw while he was thus addressing them. They seemed to feel convicted of their guilt, and sat in silence for a moment. At length, rising from her chair, said Mrs. White, "Ladies, hadn't we better be going?" Accordingly, they all at once withdrew, saying, as they left the house, they would endeavor to see him again upon this matter.

Several weeks passed without Mr. Shaw's hearing anything further of the affair, and he hoped the troublesome sisters had profited by his remarks; of course he said nothing to Mrs. Johnson about it.

One afternoon, as Mr. Shaw was writing in his study, Deacon Jones called, and, after exchanging the ordinary salutations, said he,—

"Sisters White, Wood, and Smith all called on me yesterday to enter a complaint against Sister Johnson, which, if true, ought to be examined into, and they insist that she shall be brought before the church. I directed them to you, but they said they had seen you once, and should not again."

Mr. Shaw then detailed the conversation he had with the lovely sisters, which somewhat astonished the deacon, and said he,—

"I think it would be very unwise to call Mrs. Johnson before the church; it would result in no good, and might in great evil. I will call on her, and see what she has to say; if she has been saying anything wrong of those sisters, as stated by them, or guilty of any of those immoral practices, as they represent, she may acknowledge it and ask pardon; if so, that is all that can be required of her; but, deacon, I do not believe one word of it. Is there any other flagrant sin they charge upon her?"

"Yes," said the deacon, "dancing."

"Dancing?" said Mr. Shaw. "Where, and when?"

The deacon replied, "I cannot tell anything more about it."

"Well," said Mr. Shaw, "you go and tell those women, in the first place, to clean the inside of their own platters, and then, if they know of any flagrant sin that Mrs. Johnson persists in committing, to present their charges in writing, and we will take them up at once."

With this the good old deacon left, and reported to the women as directed.

A few days after this interview the deacon called again on the pastor, and handed him a letter, of which the following is a copy:

"To the Rev. Mr. Shaw, Pastor, and Deacons Jones, Sprague, and Fish.

"Brethren :—In our zeal for the interests of the church, we have made it a point, at all times, to carefully watch the brethren and sisters of the church, as we solemnly agreed and covenanted to do, and, if possible, to find some fault with them, and especially with such as are officious, and were very forward to pray or exhort in meetings any oftener than they are justified by the rules of propriety, or who, in any manner, seem to assume to lead the people; for we do not believe a person can be a Christian, and a fit member of the church, unless he or she is humble and does not attempt to put themselves forward.

"We have watched Sister Johnson for a long time, and it has pained us to see how officious and proud she has become, and to us it is an evident sign of want of grace in her heart. We feel that it is unsafe for the church to retain such a member, for there is great danger to us all from her influences; and we charge Sister Johnson, among other sins which she delights in, with that of dancing; and we insist that an examination be had before the church.

"Truly your sisters in the church,

"Mrs. White, Wood, and Smith"

"Well," said Mr. Shaw, "this is a precious document! What do these mischief-makers want? Do they wish to break up the church? to cause dissensions and bickerings? I wish they would mind their business. Deacon, can't you persuade their husbands to send them away for a visit, and see if they will not forget their chosen occupation for awhile, and let the church have rest? But, joking aside, you call here to-morrow at two P.M, and we will go and see Sister Johnson, and learn what she has to say." With this the deacon left.

The morrow came, and, at the appointed time, Deacon Jones drove up to Mr. Shaw's, and together they rode to Mr. Johnson's, and met Mrs. Johnson, when the following conversation took place.

*Mr. Shaw.* "Sister Johnson, some of the sisters in the church have complained of you for dancing. As it is against the rules of the church, we have come to learn about it, and hear what you have to say."

*Mrs. Johnson.* "Well, sir, I really do not remember of dancing but once for years, and that was at an evening party at Mrs. Lockwood's. I spent an evening there with several friends, and, at the close of the evening, Jane Lockwood (who, you know, is a fine performer on the piano) was playing, and Mr. Lockwood invited the ladies and gentlemen to dance, and, as he was himself a member of the church (and I think no one will for a moment doubt his piety), I thought no ill of it, and danced a few moments."

"Well, were you not aware that it was contrary to the rules of the church?"

"No, sir, I was not aware that the rules of the church were so rigid as to prohibit a little innocent amusement like that; but, of course, I would not myself approve of ordinary dances; and perhaps it was wrong even in that case. But, sir, is there not something else the dear sisters are after than simply to call me to an account for so trivial an offense? If all that has been told me is true, we have some busybodies in our church who, for the good of the church, had better be out of it."

"Well, if your dancing that evening has been the cause of grief to others, or has led others into frivolities, was it not then wrong? and, in such case, do you not regret it?"

"Most certainly, sir, I do; for I endeavor to live by the rule of Paul, 'If meat cause my brother to offend, I will eat no more while the world standeth, lest I cause my brother to offend,' and if from participating in that, as I supposed, innocent pleasure, I have grieved any Christian's heart, or caused any one to stumble, I most heartily and earnestly repent of it, and beg to be forgiven."

*Deacon Jones.* "Well, Sister Johnson, I am glad to hear this; but are you willing to go before the church and make this confession?"

*Mr. Shaw.* "Deacon, we must ourselves be cautious, and not commit a greater error than Sister Johnson has. She has made all needed confession, for we have already answered the injunctions of the Scriptures and the rules of the church."

*Mrs. Johnson.* "Will you be so kind as to inform me who my complainants are, Mr. Shaw?"

"No, sister; it will do you no good, and I shall see that nothing further comes of it."

Thus ended the attempt on the part of three meddlesome, envious women to destroy the reputation and usefulness of the most efficient lady in the church.

Having completed my visit, I returned home, and soon after was taken sick, as previously stated.

During my sickness my dear father died; but I was permitted to know nothing of it until my recovery.

About this time my husband was called South on business for his house, expecting, when he left, to be absent about ten days.

After waiting the appointed time and no return, I

began to fear lest some evil had befallen him; but I hoped for the best.

Day after day I anxiously awaited his return, and my nights were passed sleepless and alone; and yet not alone, for God was with me, and I felt that I had the sympathy of the great heart of Jesus.

Have any of my readers been placed under such circumstances? A dear friend away from home and past his appointed time for return, and, after days and nights of anxious and earnest watchings and waiting, yet no tidings concerning him? If so, you can appreciate my feelings at this time. At such times it is unnatural for a person to fancy the absent friend safe; and although one's thoughts are almost continually upon them, yet we do not think of them as being detained by causes or circumstances within their control. On the contrary, it is the natural inclination of the mind to think of them as in trouble; fearful forebodings seize upon the mind at once, and we fancy all sorts of evil have come upon them. Hope seems to be driven out of the mind entirely, and if, while thus held in suspense, hope again gains the ascendency, it is wholly because of the controlling power of the will. Affections do not grow cold,—far from it; on the contrary, they become more ardent, for it is a law of one's nature that to appreciate health we must have suffered from disease; to fully appreciate blessings we must have passed through adversity. This law also holds good in the physical system. To become strong and muscular, we must not recline on beds of down, and spend our days in idleness and inactivity; but we must labor and exercise, and the more earnestly we apply this régime, the stronger and more muscular do we become. So with the attributes of the mind. In order to a spontaneous exercise of the affections to the highest degree, it is necessary

that the object of our love should be removed from us for
a time.   As with love, so with the opposite.   We never
know how to, and indeed we never do really, hate evil,
until we have learned to love the good ; and it is a merciful provision of God's grace, that he has given us the
records of the sins and backslidings of his chosen people
of old, and of the terrible judgments which came upon
them at times in consequence, and also of the patience
and faith of the old worthies "as our ensamples ;" and,
knowing that human nature has not changed, we may
thereby be enabled to shun the rock on which they
drifted.

My husband's partner in business was also greatly
alarmed for his safety, by reason of his prolonged ab-
sence, and telegraphed to places where he thought he
could reach him, but to no avail.

Oh, how I did plead with God for the safe return of
my dear husband, and the father of my dear children !
and every morning and night I would talk with them of
the possibility of evil having happened to their father,
until their little hearts would almost break.   I did not do
this to cause them unnecessary pain and anguish.   But
first, because my soul was borne down with grief, and I
felt the absolute need of a responsive expression from
some other heart, and the more ardent, the greater is the
relief which comes to the afflicted ; and this can be found
nowhere so strong as in the outbursts of the emotions of
the pure and tender heart of a child.   And secondly, because I wished to impress, upon their young and tender
hearts, truths and principles of vital importance to them ;
and under no circumstances could this be so effectually
accomplished as when in deep sorrow.   And thirdly,
because such experience would bring all our hearts nearer
together, and, let what would happen to them in after-life,

they would never forget the impressions they received at that time, and their love for me would be increased, and mine for them proportionately strengthened, and should their father return they would also love him the better for it.

Thus I took my children before the altar of God every morning and evening, and presented my petition earnestly to Him who "tempers the wind to the shorn lamb."

At length I received a letter from a gentleman in Atlanta, Georgia, saying my husband had been very sick at that place, and was still confined to his room from the effects of an injury he received some three weeks previous; but he was now gaining, and would be able to leave for home, he thought, within a week, and that he wrote by my husband's request.

I at once wrote my dear husband of the agony of mind I had endured on behalf of him, as also had our precious children, and thus I was most thankful,—yes, indeed, perfectly enraptured with the thought that he was safe, and that I should see him again. Within about one week we welcomed him home; but, alas, how changed from what he was when he left! Then, hale and hearty,—now, pale and haggard. I nursed him as none but a loving wife could, and he gradually improved until he regained his usual health. For a time he was affectionate and faithful; but it was not many months before I noticed upon his coming in of evenings the smell of ardent spirits about him, and, by degrees, he would spend his evenings away from home. I became greatly alarmed at this, and prayed most earnestly for him; and, as often as I thought prudent and safe, so as not to irritate him, and thus lose my influence entirely over him, I would beg of him to desist from those evil practices, for my sake, for his dear children's sake, and for his own happiness; and he always promised me he would, but as often violated his promises, until it really seemed to me I could not endure the trial. And my mind reverted to the time when my husband was repeating his pledges to me, and urging me to marry him, on the strength of these pledges, and the impressions I then had, as I said to my father, "that I had feared Mr. Goodspeed was not so good as he would have me believe;" and I was forced to utter the exclamation of one of old, "For my sighing cometh before I eat, and my roarings are poured out like the water. For the thing which I greatly feared is come upon me, and that which I was afraid of is come unto me."

And could my children have been mercifully taken away, I should have longed for death.

I learned from his partner that he so far neglected his business as to frequent the saloons and gambling-hells, and that unless he speedily reformed he should dissolve partnership with him. I had previously begged of my friends to lend their influence to aid me in recovering my dear husband, and several had done so. I now appealed to Mr. and Mrs. Shepherd for their aid once more; but Mr. Shepherd replied that he "knew all about him, and he felt dreadfully about it, from the fact that he had been the primary cause of my distress, by urging me first to marry Mr. Goodspeed." I replied, "My dear sir, cast no such reflections; marriages are made in heaven. And although I am now called to pass through the deep waters of distress, yet it is for a wise purpose; and in heaven, at last, we shall understand it. There are many such problems which we have no rule to solve; we cannot understand them, their solution is left for the future." And I begged of him to aid me once more in the attempt to redeem my dear husband; but he replied, "It will be of no avail,—he is lost."

These words fell like a death-knell upon my ear.

"No avail!" "He is lost!" I repeated to myself. Is he? Can it be that Jesus died for him in vain? that my intercessions, entreaties, and prayers, are all in vain? that my love, and that of my dear children, is so freely poured out for him in vain?

No, no! he will yet be reclaimed, and my heart shall cling to him.

I then returned to my home, and to my room; and oh, the anguish of my soul, as I, all alone, thought upon our former happy days, and of hopes that were now blasted forever! and I endeavored to devise some plan by which I might win him back to temperance and sobriety, and again share his affections.

But I could think of nothing which I had not already tried. I still determined with myself that I would not cease loving him, nor my care for him and my kindly services toward him.

Time passed on. One after another of my friends forsook me. I understood well the cause: my husband's drunkenness had become so notorious that he had lost the respect of our entire circle of friends. Some of my lady friends urged me to sue for a divorce. I shuddered at the very thought of it, and replied that by God's providence I was mysteriously brought to marry Mr. Goodspeed, and had promised without any mental reservation to love, honor, and respect him. True, he had also in his marriage vow pledged his fidelity to me; but his sin did not excuse me,—no; I should still continue to love him, and I felt sure that my efforts would yet be owned and blessed of God, and my husband yet be brought to see his sins in their enormity, and turn and live.

One of the reflections which caused me fearful forebodings, was that he might squander his property, and myself and children be left poor and homeless. And I took care, from the first, to see that my children were having the very best advantages for education, lest poverty might come upon us, and they, in consequence, be deprived of those blessings.

Many of my friends suggested that I apply to the courts to be protected in the property; but I would not listen for one moment to such a proposition. I replied that I would do nothing to bring my family into disrespect; I would suffer from extreme poverty rather than that my husband should be written imbecile on the public records.

# CHAPTER XIV.

As I sat in the library, mending my husband's garments, a stranger called. He said he was Deputy United States Marshal, and had business with my husband. I replied that he would probably find him at his place of business, No. —— —— Street.

"Place of business!" said he. "Is your husband a man of business?"

I replied that he was.

"Alas, my lady!" said he, "your husband has most grossly deceived you. He has no business, and has had none for a long time. He squandered his entire interest in the house of Goodspeed & Hammond long since, and the firm dissolved. He then borrowed money and mortgaged this place for all it is worth, and also the furniture in this house, and has, I am informed, spent it all in gambling, drinking, and other vices, and Mr. Hammond, Mr. Shepherd, and other friends, have for a long time supported you and your children, by sending you money and supplies through Mr. Hammond. And now I have come by order of the court to take possession of this house and furniture under the mortgage, as the debt has been long due."

"Oh, my God!" said I, "have mercy on me and my children," and I fell fainting into my chair.

At the gentleman's call my servant-girl came, and by the application of restoratives I soon recovered; upon seeing the stranger, I relapsed into my former condition,

( 159 )

and it was some moments before they could restore me. Upon seeing me safe again, he remarked :

"You are too ill, madam, to talk with further to-day. I will call at ten A.M. to-morrow."

As soon as he left, I cried, "Oh, my God, cut me off! don't let me see the light of another sun !"

My maid was frightened, and said she,—

"You're crazy, mum; I'll run for the doctor."

"No," said I, "I am not crazy, but I have sinned."

Bessie, my maid, helped me on to my bed, and gave me a cup of strong tea, and I felt somewhat revived.

But oh, the anguish of my soul ! I repented of my sin, and prayed for strength to endure the trials of a life of poverty that was before me, that myself and children might be preserved from all temptation.

For an instant, when realizing that a faithless husband had brought such suffering upon his devoted family, I felt hard toward him. But I soon rebuked myself, and said, Yes, I will continue to live with him, and God will bless me !

Night came on, and my precious children gathered about my bed. William had now grown to be a young man, and my daughters quite large girls. They were all well fitted for life (for children of their ages), except that they were strangers to adversity. They earnestly inquired the cause of my illness, and for a time I evaded their queries; but at last said I, "My dear children, you may as well know it now as to-morrow."

I then repeated the statement made by the marshal, and the girls burst into a flood of tears. William turned his face to the wall, and stood silent for a few moments, until the girls had partially assuaged their grief. Then, turning upon us his countenance all radiant with love and an expression of manly dignity, said he,—

" My dear mother, and you, my dear sisters, let us all
put our trust in God. You, mother, have long since
taught us from the Bible, that Jesus will take care of
those who put their trust in him; and though called to
pass through deep waters, yet the floods shall not over-
flow them. Then let us trust in Him, and I will be your
stay and support."

Just at this time, my husband came reeling into the
house, and, not finding me in the library as usual, he
stumbled to my bed, and with an oath, said he,—

" What are you in bed for this time of day? Get up,
and get me some tea."

I replied, " I was ill and could not."

With that he laid hold of me to take me out, and, as
quick as thought, William caught hold of him and hurled
him down upon the floor. The girls screamed; and I
cried, " My dear William, he is your father, you must not
treat him so ill."

William replied, " I don't care if he is my father, he
shall not abuse my mother."

William helped his father into the dining-room, where
the girls prepared him some tea. After tea he lay upon
the lounge, and, after dozing awhile, William related the
occurrences of the day, to which he seemed perfectly indif-
ferent. His moral sensibilities had become so benumbed
that he seemed but one remove from the brute. And yet
I could not find it in my heart to forsake him.

This was a night of sorrow, with no rest, my mind
being too greatly disturbed. I finally fell asleep and
dreamed that a man, with a haggard look, stood before
me, and screamed in my ear, " Ruined! ruined! ruined!"
I sprang up in bed, panting like a scared roe; but no one
was present, and all was still. I laid myself down again,

my temples were throbbing, neuralgia had seized upon my nervous system, and I cried, "O Lord, give to thy chosen sleep!" After tossing about for a time, I again slumbered, but only to be terrified by dreams and visions of poverty and deep distress; and thus I suffered until the morning light.

In the morning I sent William to call Mr. Shepherd. He came, and I related all to him. He replied that he was aware of it all, and both himself and his wife had dreaded this fatal day, and that he had a small house of four rooms just vacated by one of his tenants; he would that morning have it furnished, and I could take possession of it at once, and occupy it free of rent or cost as long as I chose.

I thanked him with all my heart.

"Well," said he, "how about that brute of a husband of yours? You had better let me kick him out of the house."

"Oh, sir!" said I, "don't call my dear husband a brute. I feel sure he will yet be reclaimed."

"Well," said he, "I hope he may; but I should as soon think of seeing a soul enter a wooden man, as to see him a man again."

I then went to the kitchen to inform Bessie (the kitchen-maid). Said I, "Bessie, we are ruined."

"Ruined, mum," said she; "an' sure, an' what have I done to ruin ye?"

"Oh," said I, "you have not done it. You have been a good, kind girl, and I shall always love you for the good you have done for us. But my husband has been unfortunate and lost all his property, and now this house and furniture have gone to pay debts with, and we are poor, not worth a dollar in the world, save our clothing."

She looked with astonishment as I made the statement, and exclaimed, " Ye are in a bad way, sure; what can I do for ye ?"

I replied that we were to go into a small house, belonging to Mr. Shepherd, in the alley leading off from ———— Street, and she could go with us and stay a day or two to help us wash, and after that the girls and myself must do all the work.

"An', sure," said she, "is that the house ye are going to live in,—the same that Johnny O'Neil left the day before yisterday? Bad luck to ye, an' sure an' I will go wid ye to help the ladies. I will stay wid ye, God bless ye, mum. I have lived wid ye these many years, and niver a cross word have ye uttered in my prissince; and the young ladies and William have all been very kind to me, and I'll not lave ye now ; no, indade, I won't. May the Howly Virgin protect us, I can sleep on the floor, and the young ladies will let me comb my hair before their glass, and I'll stay by ye. Neither you nor the young ladies are used to work, and yer hands 'll get sore."

" Bless your soul, Bessie," said I, " you are a good girl, and God will reward you for your kindness. But how shall I pay you? I have no money, and shall have to live upon the charities of my friends until we can get work of some sort."

" Well, mum," said she, "the ladies can all earn more by teaching than you can by housework, and I will go wid ye, and we will put in together, and I'll risk but we can live. The gintry, ye know, won't come to that house, so ye'll want no new clothes for some time."

Bessie's arguments were irresistible, and I consented to let her cast her lot with us.

And, in my reflections upon this conversation, and my knowledge of Bessie's character, I could but think, and said to myself, "How ill able we are to judge of the real character of an individual by the external appearance!"

Here was an ignorant, uncouth Irish girl, with a soul full of holy emotions, and the instant that the chord of sympathy within that soul was touched, it vibrated with heavenly music, pure, disinterested benevolence, none of the rubbish of selfishness there; and I thank God for just such a friend; and no language can express the feeling of joy which thrilled my heart as she made her simple declaration; and, relating the conversation directly after to the children in the drawing-room, I remarked that it was to me an indication of God's favor, and *labora et spera* should still be my motto. I know we shall see brighter days by-and-by, and your father will yet be reclaimed, and we saved from utter ruin and disgrace.

At precisely ten A.M. the marshal came. I had kept my husband in, and, as the marshal read him the ejectment papers, I thought I could observe a momentary expression of alarm, but he soon relapsed into his usual stupid condition.

I said to the marshal that a friend had provided us with a house, and if he would be so kind as not to give us unnecessary trouble we should leave the house in a day or two. To this he assented in a very gentlemanly manner, and before nightfall the next day we were all snugly packed away in Mr. Shepherd's little brown house in the alley leading off ——— Street.

"Alas for earthly joy, and hope, and love
　Thus stricken down e'en in thy holiest hour."

How true it is that "The heart knoweth its own bitterness."

When the heart of one is all broken down with sadness, and it seems as though that soul was alone in the world, the mind becomes beclouded, and all is dark and dismal with fearful forebodings ; then it is that we feel the need of friends, sympathizing hearts. But even though our friends may cluster around us at such times, and offer words of consolation and love, yet their sympathies cannot reach down into the inner soul and grasp the painful tumor which is gathering in the heart.

By this my readers will not understand me as undervaluing the outgushings of warm hearts, full of sympathy for the troubled and afflicted. A person who undervalues such expressions of the holiest emotions of the soul is a scandal to his species.

Immediately after moving into our humble home in the alley, William applied for and obtained a situation as second clerk in the store of Mr. Hammond, my husband's former partner, and was thus earning something for the support of the family ; and Mr. Hammond also promised him higher salary than he had paid for the same services, and, so soon as the bargain was closed, William hastened, full of joy, to inform us of his good fortune. As he came into the house, his countenance was as radiant as a sun-beam, and said he, "Mother, never fear ; I can support you and the girls. I have secured a situation in Mr. Hammond's store, which I am resolved to fill to his entire satisfaction, and I shall then be able to pay for all we need."

About this time Mrs. Shepherd called to excuse herself for not giving me a better house, but said they could not get possession of one.

Said I, "My dear friend, you need make no excuse. You and your husband have already done more for me than I have any right to' expect, and I cannot find language to express my gratitude."

On leaving, she dropped a twenty-dollar bill in my

hand. My heart was so full that I could not acknowledge it, and, covering my face, I burst into tears. Bidding me good-by, she said, "I will see you again, dear, in a day or two."

I reported the present to Bessie immediately after Mrs. Shepherd left, for, as I have before stated, we had formed a copartnership, and I was resolved to carry out the agreement to the letter.

"Well," said Bessie, "I told ye, mum, that the good Lord would take care of us ; but I don't think much of that old brute of a man of yourn."

"Oh," said I, "Bessie, don't call him a brute. He is my husband, and I am bound to treat him kindly, let him do as he will; and I feel sure he will yet reform."

"Reform!" said she. "No, indade; not so long as he can get a shilling to buy a mug of whisky wid. There ought to be a law making a damage to any one selling whisky to a drunkard."

"Yes," said I, "and there should be a law making it an offense punishable by a heavy fine for a man to sell ardent spirits to any one who fails to provide for his family."

# CHAPTER XV.

ONE day, while we were all engaged upon some work we obtained of a merchant tailor, a wagon drove to the door, having (as I observed from my window) a man lying on some straw. The driver hallooed. I went to the door, and said he, "Here, old woman, I've brought home your old man; and I guess it's about the last of him, too."

Bessie heard him, and, rushing past me, with her broom, she screamed out, "Ye dirty old spalpeen, bad luck to ye; may the Howly Virgin spit on ye, callin' my good lady the old woman. Ye desarve to be pounded, and ye does."

"Never mind, Bessie," said I; "this is part of the trials I am called to bear for some wise purpose."

"Well, sir," said I, "will you be so kind as to help my husband into the house?"

"Help," said he; "he is as dead as a door-nail, and will have to be carried in."

We all sprang for the wagon, screaming.

"Oh," said he, "don't be scared; he's only dead drunk; the old fellow will come to life again, I reckon. He hasn't all the whisky he wants yet."

We all assisted, and carried Mr. Goodspeed into the house, and laid him upon the bed; and Bessie went at him with herb tea until she relieved him of the surplus liquor. However, he lay stupid all that night, and, although we had lived in the little brown house in the

( 167 )

alley nearly a year, and been forsaken by nearly all my former fashionable friends, yet I think there was never a more painful conflict going on in my soul than during that long and wearisome night. For apparently my husband was dying, or at least rapidly approaching his death; and a flash of pleasure at the thought would suddenly come over me. And then I would plead God's forgiveness of my great sin, and that he would spare my husband's life, and convert him. Thus I agonized all that long night.

On the morrow, he came out of the torpid state in which he had lain during the night, but was too feeble to sit up.

While the girls and myself were sewing, Bessie did the housework and nursing Mr. Goodspeed. And I overheard the following conversation between them:

"Well, Bessie, aren't you sorry to see me sick in bed?"

"Good luck to ye, no, indade, I ain't. I wish, by the Howly Virgin, you were sick all the time. I'd rather take care of a dozen sick men than one drunken man; and I reckon, old fellow, ye'll git no whisky to-day, sure."

"Oh, I must have some whisky, or I'll die."

"Well, then, ye'll die; and ye might as well be counting yer beads and saying yer prayers, for sure an' ye'll not get a dhrop of whisky in this house."

"Call Mrs. Goodspeed. Tell her to send one of the girls for some liquor."

"No, indade, I shan't. If there's any chance for ye to die, may the Lord hasten it. I'd be glad to go for a coffin, but never a bit of whisky. An' ain't you ashamed o' yourself fur all the misery and suffering ye've brought on the fine family? Ye desarve the everlasting curse of the howly angels; an' ye'll get it too, if ye don't mind."

It was several weeks before my husband sufficiently

recovered so as to be able to sit up. During this time I had but little conversation with him. Several of his rough, drinking companions, hearing of his illness, called, but we would not let one of them into the house.

My object in not conversing with him was that he might have time to reflect, and I kept him a large part of the time like one in solitary confinement. I have heard it said that there is no punishment so tormenting, so terrible to endure, as to be shut up alone with nothing to do but think! think! think! and my impression is that Mr. Goodspeed experienced the pangs of a guilty conscience, for he would entreat me with tears in his eyes to stay with him; but not wishing to provoke him, and still being determined to leave him alone with his conscience and his God, I would excuse myself and get away from him. Days and weeks passed, and even months, before he so far recovered as to be able to go about the house.

In the mean time, by the aid and influence of Mrs. Shepherd, my daughter Rose had obtained a class in music, as she was an excellent performer on the piano, and understood the science of music. William succeeded admirably in the store; Bell and myself sewed evenings, and I taught a private day-school of girls; and Bessie did the housework and took care of my husband during the daytime.

Soon after moving into the little brown house in the alley, I found that on Sabbath days there were many children playing about, and I resolved that I would enter the missionary field at once. I didn't know but the parents would point to my drunken husband, and say, " Physician, heal thyself;" but I saw that God had opened a way for me to do good, and, for aught I knew, I had been brought there for this very purpose. I at once mentioned it to William and the girls, and they approved of it, and we resolved that we would open a Sabbath-school in our house the next Sunday at two o'clock P.M., as we all attended church in the morning. William said that he would go to all the houses in the alley Sunday morning and notify the people; and we all became greatly interested in anticipation of glorious results from our efforts.

My children obtained singing-books and Testaments at their morning Sabbath-school for use in our school.

Sunday morning came, and said William, "You know, mother, the Apostle Paul said he caught men with guile, and I am going to try it." So, putting on his oldest and worst-looking clothes, he went through the alley, from door to door, inviting the people to our Sunday-school that afternoon; and the result was twenty-one children and five adults the first Sabbath, and the school continued to increase from Sabbath to Sabbath; and, during my husband's long sickness, he was compelled to attend Sabbath-school every Sunday. Before we left the alley, we obtained, by subscription, sufficient to lease for a term of years a vacant lot next to our house, and erect a house that would hold a hundred or more people,—and we had it full every Sunday; and I thank God that he answered and blessed our labors to the conversion of many. And on this very spot, and from that Sabbath-school, has grown up the Eighth Ward Mission Church, now the largest in the city. Thus I feel that the blessings with which God crowned our feeble efforts there, fully compensated for all the suffering and misery we were called to endure. And there it was, also, that my dear husband first stood up before men and proclaimed himself a Christian. It is a precious spot,—hallowed ground to us.

After he had so far recovered as to be about the house,

I ventured to talk with him of the errors of his past life, which he deeply lamented, and said he, "My dear wife, I am not fit to live; I have been so ungrateful, have sunk so low in sin, and have brought my loving family into such deep disgrace, caused you the loss of friends and home, to dwell in a shanty in an alley. Oh, my God, what a sinner I am! And all this time, you, my dear, dear wife, have been so loving and kind, and my children so dutiful and respectful to a father who has brought them into such wretchedness, that I have by my evil practices and associations cultivated only the baser passions of my nature, and yet God has not cut me off, as he might, and as justice demanded. What shall I do? Is there any hope for me? As I now contemplate the awful experience from which I have had temporary relief, I long again for the hellish cup. Oh, how am I to be saved from repeating my past experiences! Is there no escape? When I am able again to go out among men, and from the restraints of my loving family, am I again to yield to the tempter, and so go down to hell? Oh, God forbid!"

We all sobbed aloud, and were so filled with grief we could not speak. After awhile, William broke the silence, and said:

"My father, you have indeed been a great sinner; but our dear mother has saved you from death and the dominion of Satan, by her earnest prayers in your behalf. Day and night she has earnestly presented your case to Jesus, and begged his mercy for you, that justice might not overtake you. And around our family altar, morning and evening, we have all poured out the sincere desires of our soul that the Holy Spirit would light up the spark of truth which lay imbedded under the rubbish of corruption in your soul. And thus that spark might be kindled into a flame of never-dying love for Jesus. Then we knew that Morgan Goodspeed would stand out a man among men, and our family again be taken back to the society of the respectable and virtuous."

I then spoke. Said I, "My dear husband, you have indeed caused me and our children deep sorrow: the intensity of my suffering you can never realize or appreciate. I do not feel at all inclined to chide you; you have been led away into temptations: I would not make you unhappy by adverting to our experiences during the past three years. And now, as God, in his infinite mercy, instead of suddenly cutting you off in your sins, has brought you low in sickness that you might have opportunity for reflection, and prolonged your sickness, that you might gain strength, morally, to resist temptation, I pray you to lay hold of the promises of Jesus. For he says that 'none who come unto him shall be cast out.' He can give you strength to resist the tempter, let him come to you in whatever guise he may; and you can obtain that strength from no other source. If you rely upon your own strength,—your own good pledges or resolves, without trusting in Jesus,—you will surely sink deeper in degradation and ruin than ever before. And now, for Jesus' sake who died for you, died in your stead, suffered for your sins, that you might be saved from everlasting torments; for your wife's sake, who left her father and friends to become yours, and did so upon the strength of your solemn pledges to remain a faithful and devoted husband so long as life should last; and for the sake of your dear children, who must carry the name of Goodspeed through life, and whose future condition in society will depend much upon your resolve to-night,—I say, in view of all these motives, and in the name of God

and humanity, I entreat you to now resolve to lead a
Christian's life from this moment!"

He then asked me to pray for him; we, for the first
time in our lives, knelt together, and I earnestly im-
plored God's mercy to rest upon my dear husband;
upon my concluding, he burst forth in an earnest prayer
and confession, and a consecration without reserve.
William followed him in a prayer of thanksgiving and
praise. Thus, by the mysterious operations of providence, was God's altar erected in the family of Morgan
Goodspeed.

My dear husband continued to improve in health from
day to day; as soon as he was able, he called on
some of his old drinking companions, and succeeded in
bringing them into my Sabbath-school; and, before we
left there, God gave us the satisfaction of knowing that
many of them were converted from the error of their
ways, and became useful members of society; one young
lawyer, of fine talents and education, but who had led
a dissolute life, was so filled with love for Jesus, and
burning desire for the salvation of men, that he became
a self-constituted city missionary and preacher, and was
most successful in his labors. Our former friends, learning of the conversion of my husband, and of his activity
and zeal in his efforts for good, again gathered about us,
and were solicitous to aid him in his efforts to again es-
tablish himself in business.

By invitation of Mr. Hammond, Mr. Goodspeed entered
his store as salesman by commission instead of a salary,
well knowing that his abilities as a salesman were such
that he could make more money than by a salary; he
found that he could sell more goods after he became a
Christian than ever before.

15*

When he had been with Mr. Hammond about six months, the latter proposed to retire from active business, and give it into the hands of my husband and William, by selling them an undivided half of the stock on credit, charging them six per cent. on that capital, and dividing the profits equally. This was done at once, and the old sign of Goodspeed & Hammond, that for over three years and a half had lain in the store loft, was pulled out of the rubbish, cleaned up, and raised to its old place at No. —, Milk Street, Boston.

The business of the firm was prosperous; the times were propitious. Many of my husband's old customers, who were so because of their especial friendship for him, and who had left the house after his failure, now learning of his reform, and that he had resumed business, came back to the house to trade, and his business rapidly increased.

My husband was anxious to locate his family in a more respectable house and neighborhood, but I declined until he and William should be able to purchase a home. Our expenses were light, for I still continued to teach, as did also Rose, and we were slow to go back into society, preferring to be urged back, than to crowd ourselves upon our friends who had forsaken us in our adversity.

At the close of the first year the books of the firm showed large profits to Mr. Goodspeed and William's account, and one more year of equal prosperity would entirely wipe out their indebtedness, and place them one-half owners of the immense stock, which result was achieved.

One morning, as Mr. Goodspeed entered the counting-room at the store, William called his attention to an advertisement of a beautiful house and splendid furniture, on —— Street, No. —, for sale at auction, at ten A.M. of that day.

Said my husband, "William, would you like to have me purchase back my old home, the house in which my precious children were born?"

"Yes, indeed," said William; "and if it is known that you want it, it will go cheap; and we can spare sufficient to meet the cash payment. I wonder if it is the same house and furniture that we left?"

"Come with me," said his father, "and we will see."

They accordingly went to the house, and found it the same, and apparently just as we left it, furniture and all, for that had been kept well covered.

William afterward informed me that his father was so overcome, upon entering the house, that he sat down in the same easy-chair he used to occupy so much, and wept like a child. My husband attended the auction, and, so soon as people learned that Morgan Goodspeed desired to purchase his old home, they ceased bidding entirely, and the house and furniture were sold, and immediate possession given; but the deed and bill of sale were both made to Mrs. Aspasia Goodspeed.

On the morrow, after the purchase of the old mansion, my husband remarked at the breakfast-table, that he had the day before purchased a house on —— Street, in the neighborhood of where we used to live, and directed us to be ready to move into it by ten A.M., which we could do, as we had no furniture to move, and he said he purchased furniture with the house.

At ten we were ready, and husband and William came for us.

As we were passing along street after street, I remarked it was the first carriage-ride I had enjoyed for over four years.

After reaching our old neighborhood, I watched the horses eagerly to see where they were to stop. At last we were driven to the gate of our old mansion, and hastened into the house. We strolled through it more as an explorer would through the chambers of the buried cities of the Old World, than as people who had come to dwell there.

Wonder and astonishment filled our minds. We were amazed and confounded. The past seemed to me like a dream.

I sank down upon a sofa in the parlor. My husband sat beside me just as he used to formerly. Said I, "Morgan Goodspeed, is this a dream?"

"No," said he; "but it is another manifestation of God's love;" and, drawing some papers from his pocket, and handing them to me, said, "My dear wife, I have purchased this house and all this furniture in your name, and now present you the title-papers. Whatever will again occur, you will have a home."

Can any of my readers appreciate my feelings at this announcement? If so, well, it relieves me; for I could not find language to express them.

Bessie stood by and heard it all; and, after waiting for me to speak, and finding I did not, she wiped the tears from her eyes, and said she, "Mr. Goodspeed, the last time I saw ye in this house I wouldn't a given a haight for ye; and it's only for the prayers and kindness of my good lady that ye are alive at all at all. And ye have dun a blessed thing to give the good lady the house and furniture; but couldn't ye do a little something fur me, jist to remember me by,—a calico dress, or something, jist because we have all got back into this house again,—and I went with the ladies, and I staid wid 'em, and sure and I'm glad I did?"

Said my husband, " Bessie, you have been a good girl; now you ought to get married and have a home."

"An' sure an' haven't I a home here, sir?" said she.

" Yes," replied my husband, " but you should have one of your own now. If you will marry Johnny Scates (and you know he wants you to), I will purchase that house we have just moved out of, and the furniture also, and give them to you."

" Will ye?" said she; and her eyes sparkled like diamonds. " Well, by the Howly Virgin, I'll do it this very night, an' sure an' I will."

"Well done," said the girls; "go and hunt up your fellow and bring him around here, and you shall be married in this parlor." At that she flew out of the house, as a scared bird leaves its nest.

Presently, Mr. and Mrs. Shepherd, learning that we had purchased and repossessed our old home, called to congratulate us upon our prosperity. And Mr. Good-speed related the conversation he had with Bessie, and his proposition; and Mr. Shepherd said he would make out a deed for her, but would not take anything from us for it, and that himself, wife, and daughters would be down in the evening to attend the wedding.

Evening came, and with it Father Hagan, the priest, Johnny Scates, and some half-dozen of his friends. Mr. and Mrs. Shepherd and daughters, with all of our family, were in our elegant parlors, that were most brilliantly lighted. In the presence of these witnesses, Johnny and Bessie stood up together and were made one. And when the old priest pronounced them married, she giggled right out, and turning to Johnny, said she, " I've got a house, I have."

" Hist, girl," said Johnny : "the praste ain't through."

As soon as the ceremony was performed, Mr. Goodspeed complimented Bessie in high terms, and enjoined upon Johnny to be a faithful husband to her. He then presented her the deed to the house, and a bill of the furniture, and full receipt. And the company withdrew.

Thus ended our celebration of the reoccupancy of our old home.

# CHAPTER XVI.

"Thus drifting afar to the dim, vaulted caves
  Where life and its ventures are laid,
The dreamers who gaze, while we battle the waves,
  May see us in sunshine or shade.
Yet true to our course, though our shadow be dark,
  We'll trim our broad sail as before,
And stand by the rudder that governs the bark,
  Nor ask how we look from the shore."

My readers, I am sure, will admit that my life, up to this period, has been an eventful one.

At times I have basked in the sunshine of life, with hosts of friends about me, in the enjoyment of all the virtuous pleasures, seemingly, which wealth could afford, and with all the opportunities for self-culture through position and the influence of the society of the refined and good.

At other times my frail bark has been tossed about on the waves of adversity which seemed about to engulf me. Loss of all earthly possessions, forsaken of friends, compelled to live in the society of the poor, degraded, and outcast of the world, and yet, although drifting about upon the billows of life, my humble bark kept right on her way, true to the rudder. And when the storms were the severest, I anchored the firmer to the rock Christ Jesus, and was upheld until the storm had passed.

God, in his merciful providence, had vindicated my faith, and that, too, in a most wonderful manner.

My husband was now a devoted Christian, and gave

( 179 )

evidence of his sincerity by works of love. He became an active member in the church, and continued, during the remainder of his life, to superintend the mission Sabbath-school, in the alley, which I established, and where he first performed public Christian duties, and God crowned his efforts with success.

Years passed on, and my husband and William continued prosperously in business; at length they purchased the interest of Mr. Hammond, and established the firm of Goodspeed & Son.

About this time my daughter Rose married the Rev. Mr. Scott, who was ordained a missionary to the Indies, whither they went at once; and I am pleased to know that very many of the benighted heathens have, through their instrumentality, been brought from Nature's darkness into the glorious light and liberty of the Gospel of Christ.

The day of Rose's marriage was also the occasion of William's wedding; thus, as I gave one, Providence gave me another, as if it were decreed that I should not again be required to lessen the number of my sympathizing friends.

My daughter Bell graduated at the —— Seminary, and although Mr. Goodspeed possessed ample means for us to live in affluence, Bell said she chose not to live a passive or useless life, consequently accepted a situation as first assistant teacher in the very same seminary from which I graduated when a girl.

The seasons, in quick and rapid succession, succeeded each other, and I felt that time was fast passing away.

It was evening; my husband and myself were seated in the library alone; a fearful storm was raging without; the slats in the shutters were flapping, to keep time to the Æolian music of the winds, and all was dismal, dreary, and dark; but the angel of love presided at our quiet fireside.

Removing his spectacles, and laying aside his evening paper, he addressed me as follows :

" Well, wife, I really feel as though I was about through with life, and very soon will have to bid adieu to earth, and enter upon the realities of an unseen world."

" Why do you feel so ?" I inquired. " You are not ill, are you ?"

" No, I am not; but when I realize how rapidly time is passing away, the seasons coming and going with a velocity increasing with my years, it is an evidence to me that my work is about done,—and, oh, such a work! As I look back upon my life, a large part of which has been misspent, it causes me deep grief, and since, through God's infinite mercy, I was taken from the depths of degradation, and my soul filled with heavenly desires, and God's special providence manifested toward me, and my precious family subsequently, I feel like exclaiming, throughout all eternity, ' Grace! grace ! all grace !'

" But in his economy God works through human instrumentalities, and I firmly believe that he raised you up on purpose for my conversion; for few, if any, would have continued faithful before the mercy-seat as you have ; and, in eternity, the next theme to that of a Saviour's dying love for which I shall tune my harp of praise and songs of everlasting joy, will be that God in his infinite mercy chose you, my dear wife, a messenger of heavenly love, and that by your faith, love, prayers, and good works, you were instrumental in snatching me from the horrible pit, and planting my feet upon the rock Christ Jesus."

For moments the deep emotions of my soul choked my utterance ; at length, gaining relief through my crying, I replied :

"The ways of God are mysterious. I am entitled to no credit for having performed my duty toward you. I had, all through our adversity and deep distress, abiding faith in Christ's promises, and was determined to test their validity by the constancy of my purpose; and, as by the exercise of our physical system the muscles all gain vigor and strength, so it is with the attributes of the mind; hence the fruits of my faith were manifested in kindly deeds toward you, calculated to soften the asperities of your mind, and render you more likely to yield your stubborn will to the influences of the Holy Spirit, and thus, also, was my faith in God manifested by my efforts for the good of others. I know full well that He who had promised to 'feed the young ravens when they cry,' would not turn a deaf ear to a confiding soul."

After our evening worship we retired for the night.

But a few weeks passed and my husband was taken violently sick with fever. He had previously had such attacks, and I hoped to throw it off. But, alas, it was not so to be! He continued to grow worse through the night, and for days after he was quite low.

I felt impressed that this was to be his last sickness, and the thought of his being taken, and I left, caused me deep distress.

I went to my closet and shut the door; and there alone with my Saviour, where in former years I plead earnestly for my erring husband, I now prayed that this cup of affliction, if consistent with his will, might pass from me; otherwise, that I might be prepared to endure it.

At last the physician informed me that Mr. Goodspeed could not recover, but that I must not alarm him by informing him of it.

"My dear sir," I replied, "he will not be alarmed at all. He is ready to die at any time; but how can I endure it?"

As I came to the bedside, he observed I had been weeping.

"Oh," said he, "my dear wife, weep not for me. I am only going home a little while—just a little while—before you, that's all!"

Our pastor called frequently during his illness; and at one of his last visits he inquired of Mr. Goodspeed, "On what grounds do you hope for salvation?"

My husband replied, "Not by any works of righteousness that I have done, but by the sovereign mercy and grace of God, through Jesus Christ my Saviour."

"But," said the pastor, "are you not to be credited in God's book of records with the good you have done?"

My husband replied, "Not at all; I am to be credited nothing in my account with God; it is all debit on my side of the account. I have forfeited all right to a credit with him, and he had determined to thrust me into the prison of endless despair, as he knew full well I never could repay the debt; for it was his inexorable law that the debt must be paid, or the debtor be everlastingly punished. Seeing this, the great heart of Christ was moved with pity in my behalf, and he paid the debt for me; hence the account has been transferred to Jesus, and my indebtedness is to him."

"Well, then, how do you expect to square your account with Jesus?"

"I do not expect to at all. I never can pay it, nor any part of it. I am a bankrupt sinner; but I have not the least fears in going into the august presence of Jesus; for I know he will freely forgive the debt I owe, and welcome me into his presence as though I had never sinned. For he says, 'Come unto me, all ye who labor and are heavy-laden, and I will give you rest.' I was heavy-laden with the burdens of sin, and by the influences of the Holy Spirit yielded myself to Jesus, and he rolled the burden off from my soul at once, and I became dead to sin. 'Now, if we be dead with Christ, we believe that we shall also live with him.' 'Therefore, being justified by faith, we have peace with God through our Lord Jesus Christ.' What more do I need? Jesus says, 'My blood cleanseth from all sins,' and his 'Spirit witnesses with my spirit, that I have been born again.' I feel my utter unworthiness and helpless condition, and shall go into the presence of my Saviour naked and poor; but I believe to become rich in that heavenly inheritance prepared for me."

The pastor replied, "Brother Goodspeed, you need none of my counsel or advice; you are taught by one higher than I. The Holy Spirit has indeed manifested his presence to you, and clearly revealed himself and your duty. And oh that I may be permitted to see my last days with my faith as clear, and firmly centering on Christ as is yours! Have you any message for the church?"

"Yes," my husband replied; "tell the brethren to exercise stronger faith in Jesus, and to let their faith be more ardent, to put away evil-speaking from among them, and wicked surmisings; remembering that if they speak ill of a brother and wound his conscience, it is a wound inflicted upon the great heart of Christ himself, and is a fearful sin to be answered for. Tell them they must not judge one another, for with what judgment they judge, they too will be judged. They must remember that if poor, sinning, weak mortals cannot forgive and overlook each other's imperfections, how can we expect pardon from the great God. I wish you would endeavor to impress more forcibly the truth, that a backbiter and an evil-speaker is only revealing his own character; and, knowing this, every Christian, when evil thoughts arise in his mind, should at once rebuke the evil spirit which prompts them, and at the same time cultivate and cherish the opposite feeling. By this process of educating himself, he will grow in grace, and be strengthened to resist evil thoughts and desires, and overcome the evil propensities of his nature, and thus grow up into the full stature of a perfect man in Christ Jesus."

On the morning of the day of my husband's death, I observed a strange expression of countenance upon him, with his eyes intently fixed upon the ceiling, and a terrible scowl upon his face. After awhile it would pass off, and his face would wear a smile. Then again despair seemed to seize hold of him. I felt sure a terrible conflict was going on in his soul. It seemed like a violent storm-cloud passing over the earth, when the forest is beaten down in its path, and, after it has passed, the sun shines out in all its loveliness and splendor.

After enduring the conflict a long time, he burst out with the following,—

> "I stand on Zion's mount,
>   And view my starry crown;
> No power on earth my hope can shake,
>   Nor hell can thrust me down."

Before the sun had gone down in the western horizon, my husband had entered upon the realities of an unseen world, and I was left alone.

Thus was I brought to widowhood; which, for a Christian, is the nearest relation to God to which a human being can be brought. For he says, "I will be the widow's God."

Weeks passed on: I felt lonely and sad; yet happy in the thought that my dear husband had gone to dwell where trouble can never come, but where he will bask in the sunlight of Christ's love forever, and that I should ere long be permitted to join him and strike the notes of praise on our golden harps together.

I was left with a large property, and was thus enabled to bestow my charities with a liberal hand. I employed at my own cost never less than five, and as many as ten, colporteurs, constantly distributing books and tracts, and supplying the poor with food, and providing homes for the outcast.

My daughter Bell had now married and moved West. William continued the business at the old house. By this time his eldest son had entered the store, and William continued the business under the old sign of Goodspeed & Son.

# CHAPTER XVII.

" Every family is a history within itself, and even a poem, to those who know how to read its pages."

Philosophers have declared that intellectual recreation is needful to the well-being and mental health of man.

Pindar said, " Rest and enjoyment are universal physicians."

Aristotle says, " It is impossible for men to live in continual labor: repose and games must succeed to cares and watching."

Solomon inquires, " Who knoweth what is good for a man in this life,—all the days of his vain life which he spendeth as a shadow ?"

Socrates said, " The highest degree of happiness was attainable only by doing good to our fellow-men, by leading our youth in paths of virtue, and thus we should propitiate the gods and secure their approbation, and insure ourselves immortal pleasures in the spirit-world."

The Assembly's Catechism says, " The chief end of man is to glorify God and enjoy him forever."

Now, in my view, neither of the foregoing propositions are wholly correct, though they all contain truth, which, like all truth, is valuable.

In the first place, no antidote for a burdened heart or a diseased mind can be of any real value, unless in its effect it brings permanent relief; and as we are told by the thoroughly scientific physician that certain medicines may be given to counteract the immediate effects of the disease, but it will soon return again, and each time with increasing power; while other medicines may be administered, the effects of which will be permanent, because they are (as termed) constitutional: the entire system is thus renovated and health permanently restored.

Thus the mind of an individual may be overburdened with the cares of life, or may be oppressed with responsibilities, or may become clouded and gloomy under the trials of affliction or adversity, and temporary relief (and only temporary) may be found in "intellectual recreation," or, as Pindar says, "enjoyments," or, as Aristotle says, in "games."

Yet, after all, from the fact that the same remedies have to be so often repeated, they ultimately lose their qualities of producing even temporary relief.

We therefore need a remedy that shall prove a specific and bring permanent relief.

Socrates says, "Do good to our fellow-men, by leading our youth in paths of virtue, and thus propitiate the gods."

The Presbyterian says, "Glorify God and enjoy him forever."

Let us harness these two propositions together, and we have a perfect antidote, for Jesus has told us plainly that inasmuch as we have administered blessings to others we have done it to him, and for one to sell all that he had, and give to the poor, he would have treasure in heaven.

It is written, "It is more blessed to give than to receive."

This is an invariable law of our being. No man loves to beg, none loves to be placed in circumstances where he must be provided for by charity; but, on the contrary, there is a real pleasure in being able to bestow bounties upon others. There is no exception to this rule; it is universal; and even the miser unconsciously yields to such emotions at times. This truth being established, the proposition of Socrates is correct, and is in harmony with the injunction of our Lord, "to love our neighbors as ourselves." And by deeds of charity and love toward our fellow-men, we glorify God, because we are fulfilling his laws and elevating them above the world; and they are becoming better fitted for servants of Jesus, for spreading abroad the eternal truths of righteousness and true holiness.

I do not like the last clause in the Assembly's proposition which I have quoted: it sounds too selfish; but, when coupled with those other truths as above, it works in complete harmony; for it is God's glory that man should be redeemed and saved, and enjoy everlasting pleasures beyond the grave.

There is still another aspect in which I will view this subject, aside from the express command of God, "To do unto others as we would have them do unto us." I propose to show that these are obligations which grow out of our very natures. And what was the primary cause of the issuing of that divine command?

In the record of the Creation, we find God "made man of the dust of the ground, and breathed into his nostrils the breath of life, and he became a living soul."

Further on in the record, we find that from the man God took a woman.

We are told by our blessed Lord, "That in heaven they neither marry nor are given in marriage, but are as the angels of God," clearly implying that there is no such thing as sex in souls or spirits; and hence it is that all through Scripture the commands of God are given to

men, never to women, and woes and judgments are pronounced against men always, against women never.
Now, this is not against the male in contradistinction
from the female; but because God has created but one
man and one soul, and all other souls are the product of
that soul; have grown out of it, sprang from it, born of
it, begotten by it, as have all bodies from that first physical system.

Hence it was that Jesus must be begotten of the
Holy Spirit, or the inclinations of his soul would have
been evil.

And hence it is that we all partake of our first parents'
nature.

The woman was of the man; nowhere does it say that
God breathed into her, and she became a living soul. And
why not? Because, as I have said, but one soul was
created, and the woman's soul was born of the man's
soul. We are told that the soul which God created was
in his likeness, and as the man's physical system was
daguerreotyped in the woman, so also did she partake
of the attributes of his soul. Therefore we have but one
first parent; hence it was the curse fell upon *the man.*

"And the Lord God said, Behold, the *man* is become
as one of us, to know good and evil. Now, lest *he* put
forth *his* hand and take also of the tree of life and eat and
live forever," etc. All this is spoken of *the man,* which
would have been an incongruity had there been two independent created souls.

Now, then, reasoning from this stand-point, our souls
are all begotten, as are our bodies. It is an immutable
law of nature that like begets like, and every animal
generates its own species: so a father begets a son in his
own likeness, mentally, morally, and physically. He may
not be a perfect duplicate of his father, neither was Adam

of God, yet made in God's likeness: so the leading char-
acteristics of the father's mind are portrayed in the life of
the son. And we expect the son to be like the father: if
the father has a burning thirst for strong drink, we expect
the son will be a drunkard; if the father is a Sabbath-
breaker, we expect the son will lead a life of vice and
crime; on the contrary, if the father cultivates all the
nobler and holier attributes of the soul, we look for a
still greater development of those heavenly graces in the
child.

Therefore it is that our neighbor is our brother. as
souls, living, immortal, intelligent souls, all having
sprang from one, we necessarily partake, in a large degree, of the same properties of mind.

It should therefore be our highest aim, so far as this
life is concerned, to do all we possibly can to elevate our
fellow-men, to cultivate all their virtuous desires, to check
all baser passions, and thus fit them and ourselves for
usefulness in this life, and a glorious immortality in the
future.

I would have my readers learn from my experience
that an undying faith in God will carry them safely
through all troubles, trials, and afflictive dispensations of
providence; and, although the clouds of adversity may
gather around you dark and thick, at times, yet if your
eye of faith is intently fixed on Jesus, you will ere long
see the bright beams of heavenly light shining through
the darkness.

As I review my past life, I am a wonder to myself, a
perfect enigma, and one that human reason cannot solve:
philosophy affords no satisfactory solution; but Jesus
solves it all by saying, "As my Father hath sent me
into the world, so have I sent you into the world."

If it shall prove that I have been instrumental in

strengthening the weak faith of one, in leading an erring one back to the paths of virtue ;

Of bringing comfort or consolation to the wounded heart of an afflicted one ;

Of restoring lost hopes to one struggling in the deep waters, and against the billows of adversity ;

Of prompting the youth to noble deeds of love and good works,—

Then I shall not have labored in vain.

www.ingramcontent.com/pod-product-compliance
Lightning Source LLC
Chambersburg PA
CBHW030555040726
47497CB00008B/2735